THE BEAST
OF
MOSCOW
3

THE
BEAUTY
WHO
LOVED
HIM

BETHANY-KRIS

Published by Bethany-Kris

www.bethanykris.com

ISBN 13: 978-1-989658-54-3

Editor: Elizabeth Peters

Cover Design © Bethany-Kris

For every woman who loves a beast.

CONTENTS

1.

"Vera Avdonin, I love you to death but I swear to God if you don't answer your phone—"

She didn't even hear the rest of her mother's voicemail before deleting it because frankly, the first three seconds were enough to tell Vera that it wasn't any different than the previous three she had already heard. Just like the first handful of text messages in a string that had come in over the night while Vera's phone charged on her bedside, turned off as it had died on the ride home after being discharged from the hospital. They held the same panicked desperation.

And the reason why—Demyan had yet to call his wife, which he should have done the second he landed in Russia, according to Claire and the texts and voicemails her mother left for Vera, he had still yet to contact her.

Maybe she should have turned it on the day before once she had it plugged into the wall. Yet, after she had settled into her villa, and took the time to care for the plants that desperately needed water, and rotated for the ones that were in the windows, well … why lie? Vera forgot about the phone, and the fact she promised to call Hannah back as soon as she got home.

Never mind Claire in New York.

It was late by then. The first time since her childhood bedtimes ended when she went to bed before eight in the evening.

It all caught up.

All of it.

Vera tried to soothe her guilt with those thoughts as she shakily dialed Claire's international number and paced back and forth in front of her kitchen sink. It took her mother too many rings before she answered, and the groggy, confused voice on the other end damn near broke Vera's heart.

"Y-yeah, Demyan—hello?"

"Ma?"

Vera's pacing finally came to a standstill. At least, for the entire four seconds she counted that it took for Claire to realize it wasn't her missing husband on the other end of the call. Despite all the valid reasons her mother would have to blame Vera for her confusion, like missing every frantic phone call and message over the evening and night, Claire cursed herself.

"I knew I shouldn't have laid down. I couldn't keep my eyes open," came the regretful croak from Claire. "Have you heard from him yet? Vera, it's been more than a—"

"I only missed calls and texts from you, Ma."

And a couple from Hannah, but her friend was fine and safe in Italy at the moment. Shaken and confused

2

about her feelings regarding the recent discovery of her ex-husband's body in the canal, sure, but that was to be expected. Nonetheless, the same couldn't be said about Vera's father's current whereabouts.

"You're sure he didn't have extra layovers or an unexpected stop—"

"Vera," her mother cut in fast, the desperation leaking back into her high pitch, "he should be there *now*. Yesterday! I should have already gotten a call from him telling me he was standing on your doorstep and that I was right!"

Vera blinked. "About what?"

It took Claire more than a few passing seconds to whisper her answer. "That he was overreacting to all of this. I thought you were fine."

"I am," she tried to assure.

It did little to help her mother.

"Yes, you say that now, but Vera, where is my *husband*? Just who have you gotten yourself mixed up with there?" Claire didn't even give her stepdaughter the chance to answer, although it wasn't like Vera had one at the ready; it wasn't that simple. "I told him not to go alone! I knew he shouldn't just blindly *go*. This is horrible!"

She didn't want to work Claire up any more than her mother already was, but she had to be sure about one thing. "You're absolutely positive he should have already arrived in Russia?"

"He did!"

"Ma, just calm—"

"Vera, I've talked to his pilot. I know where he is."

She winced at the mistake.

Claire stumbled over her correction, mumbling around a sob, "Where he *should* be."

Oh, God.

That's how she was sure Vaslav knew Demyan had arrived without her delivering the news. *Who else could make her father disappear from practically thin air?* She couldn't even consider something else might be going on because Demyan wouldn't put his wife through any suffering, certainly not the fear that he was *missing*.

Claire had continued her nonsensical, panic-induced rambling. Verbally running through the last couple of days since Demyan's jet left the states and even, what his plan had been before. Only one thing really concerned Vera enough to interrupt her mother.

"It's not like I could call Roman to help. He'll lose it, Vera. Maybe Koldan could—"

"No," Vera jumped in fast. Even her loose-cannon, wild-to-his-core younger brother, by six years, would be better than her uncle, Koldan. The New Jersey bratva boss was loyal to a fault to Demyan Avdonin, but Vera seriously doubted a man like Vaslav would appreciate someone else he might consider a problem coming to his territory on her father's behalf. Blood, on the other hand, he might understand.

"Let's not call anyone right now," Vera added after a moment.

Too long of one, though.

In the next breath, her mother replied, "You better tell me why you think that's the right choice, and be quick about it, Vera. My patience is running seriously thin."

The disappointment bled into Claire's words, and Vera didn't mind that her mother didn't try to hide it.

"I know as much as you," Vera replied honestly, "but if you give me a few hours, I could probably explain a lot more."

A disgruntled squeak crackled through the speakers.

"Well, it's going to take me—"

"Vera, you or your father have five hours—five, that's it—to get him on the phone with me, or the next jet I get chartered will be for me," Claire said, every word clipped and fiery into the phone. "And whoever else I choose to bring along. I am not above making a scene. Do you understand? Pass the message along to … *whoever.*"

Right.

Whoever needed to hear it. Vera understood perfectly well.

"He won't hurt my father."

Vaslav *agreed.*

"Why can't you say that like you believe it?" her mother asked.

*

Vera hadn't even been awake long enough to brush her teeth when she finally called Claire, so by the time she was presentable enough to leave her house, without even grabbing as much as a black coffee to fill the grumbling void in her stomach, the time had crawled past nine. Locking her villa, she spun around in the cable knit, grey sweater dress to find an empty street.

Well, not entirely.

The black, sporty coupe with windows tinted opaque all the way around except the front windshield sat where Kiril had parked it the day before. Along the side of the road at the very end of her driveway.

He assured her the vehicle would still be there in the morning. His special way of letting her know that even if she didn't see him, the kid wasn't too far away. Her new babysitter, hilarious considering she was almost positive he wasn't even of legal adult age, didn't mess around about his job.

Keeping an eye on her, that was.

Whoever provided him with the new wheels, likely Igor or Vaslav, was the newest bonus he pointed to when Vera asked where he planned to sleep considering he still refused to enter her villa. Unless he was leaning into a window. The little puke enjoyed that too much.

He was still just a kid, though.

One that shouldn't be sleeping in a car.

Vera took two steps down the front steps of her villa after locking up, thinking Kiril might be sleeping in the two-door car he had sworn to her would be glittering with chrome by the end of the month, but froze when she heard a low *shit* hissed from her right.

Fast enough to make the world around her spin, she glanced to her right, seeing nothing and no one, and then left into the quiet front property of Mr. Anatoly's villa. Someone had thought to water the bushes lining the fence as she could still see the water droplets on the leaves, and the hose her neighbor had once used with the long attachment to reach his hanging plants hadn't been hung up with patience considering the extra loops of hose that remained on the ground.

"I don't think I gave them too much water, right?"

That earlier curse made a lot more sense when Vera looked to her right once more and this time, actually paid attention. While her villa and the one that belonged to Mr. Anatoly were twins in architectural design, the one to her right differed in one aspect on the outside. The front stoop greeted guests from the side and featured a closed alcove that was only visible to its neighbors and not people walking by on the street.

There stood a sheepish Kiril in the hidden alcove of her neighbors' villa. A young couple who visited their villa occasionally throughout the year when they took time away from their country home and business; he was a dentist in an area that made travel into the city difficult, so he had a large clientele. More interesting was the sharp pick-like tool that Kiril didn't even bother to hide dangling from his left hand.

"Are you trying to break into their house?" Vera asked him.

Kiril popped his tongue off the roof of his mouth before replying, "Plausible deniability. I was checking stuff out while things got a little boring."

"Kiril!"

"And I already aced your other neighbor's locks, so," he added lower. "But he's dead, and there's not much else to see in there."

Good God.

"Kiril, you can't break into people's places just because you're bored. Download a streaming service or something on your phone, okay? Just—"

"I thought you didn't have any plans today?"

His question, likely only meant to divert her from shouting at him while the rest of the street listened in on the action, brought Vera back to the bigger issue at hand. One she expected Kiril to help with whether he liked it or not.

"Did he take my father?" she demanded.

Kiril's dark, thick eyebrows shot up, making his boyish features all the more innocent when he said, "I don't know what you're talking about."

Vera grabbed onto the railing of her steps, and leaned over the edge, pointing at Kiril. "Don't play games with me. I'll call a cab, go to Vaslav and ask him myself, and you can follow behind for all I give a damn."

"That's not very nice."

He sounded genuinely upset.

Or at the very least, hurt.

Vera wished she had time for his feelings. Maybe she was spending too much time with Vaslav Pashkov.

Kiril added, "I like driving with you. You don't tell me I talk too much."

That softened Vera's anger.

Not by much.

"Did he take my father or not?" she asked.

Kiril sucked air through his grimacing mouth, and the long pause between his non-verbal response, and the words that finally came out of his mouth didn't make the situation any better. "I don't really know."

"Kiril!"

"Well!" His hands shot up, one still holding the lock picking tool, in peace. "Really, I don't!"

"What *do* you know, then?"

Because clearly, he knew something.

Kiril shrugged, and dropped his hands back down to his sides. "Just that if you call a cab, it's gonna take like two hours to get you to Dubna. I can make it there in half that as long as we beat the noon rush."

Well …

She gestured between him and the coupe parked on the side of the street. "Let's go. Move, you're the one with the keys."

*

Vera wasn't even able to enjoy the view like she usually would as Kiril drove up the long, winding driveway leading straight to the looming home on the top of the hill. The panic that had been steadily growing inside now simmered under her surface as Kiril parked.

Despite what her mother said, Vera *did* believe what she said about Vaslav. He told her that he wouldn't hurt her father as long as she had agreed to be married to him by the winter, and she expected him to follow through on that. Even if her agreement to his proposal didn't exactly come with her own set of terms.

It shouldn't need to.

Right?

"Ah, fuck," Kiril muttered when he'd shut the engine off and shot a look toward the wide stone stairs leading up to the woman waiting at the front door. "She's gonna mother me to death again. Tell her I'm not allowed to come inside, Igor said or some shit, okay?"

Vera scowled at the kid in the front seat, but he pretended like he didn't notice where she sat right next to him. "Stop it, the very least you could do is let her care. What, she makes sure you're fed while you're around and not wearing jeans with the knees blown out of them."

She knew because he told her as much.

The kid really did talk a lot. Just not about things that Vera sometimes wanted him to, for that matter.

"Hey, I like my jeans with the holes in the knees, okay?"

"Tell her that, then."

Kiril's responding facial expression didn't exactly agree. Neither did the quick shake of his head. He eyed the empty driveway, saying, "I need to call Igor. He's supposed to be here all day."

"That's a more valid excuse to stay in the car, for the record," Vera pointed out before making her exit from the passenger side. She didn't wait for his response before shutting the door on whatever Kiril was about to say, either.

She eyed the line of terracotta pots full of the same shrub she had left at home in varying degrees of growth and greenery. *When did Vaslav plan to plant those?*

Mira was already smiling in her kind way when Vera reached the steps and took the first few two at a time.

"I saw Kiril when he was opening the gate and already called Mr. Pashkov up from the back for you, Miss—"

"Could you just call me Vera?" she asked, hating to interrupt Mira but knowing it also needed to be said.

Mira pursed her lips, and keeping her hands neatly folded at her front, bobbed a bit on the spot in response. "Informally, I suppose I can."

Vera raised a brow.

"And I will," Mira quickly added. Then, she leaned sideways to look beyond Vera the higher she came on the stairs. "Is Kiril coming in?"

"Maybe later. He's got other things to handle right

now."

And that was the most she would lie for the kid, too.

Mira nodded, but the way her mouth pinched in a tight smile said she wasn't entirely happy about it. Vera almost wondered … did she want to be a mother—was that why she mothered Kiril whenever the young man was within breathing distance of her?

"Anyway," Mira said, "Mr. Pashkov said he would be up from the lake soon. I don't know what he's been doing all night down at the guesthouse, but it's better than him pacing the halls here."

Vera's brow furrowed as she came to stand beside Mira on the top of the steps. She'd left the front door open a few inches, but there was no sign of the black retriever that had been using the steps as a makeshift bed the last time she stood there.

"Is he not sleeping well?" she asked the older woman.

That question had Mira glancing away. "Better for you to ask him that. He said he'd meet you in the dining room, lunch is nearly ready. Are you hungry?"

Her stomach must have heard the prodding. It grumbled accordingly, and the empty ache the rumble left behind was enough to make Vera nauseous.

"I could eat," she replied.

"Good. I made too much Olivier salad. He wanted something with chicken today."

Mira gestured Vera to the front door, and made small talk as the two headed inside. She didn't ask Vera to remove her boots at the entrance rug, but rather, brushed off the bit of dirt as expected and ushered her across the space to the small vestibule leading into the large dining room. It wasn't a space she'd spent much time in other than to cross through to reach the kitchen, but she knew it well enough to spot the difference the second she stepped inside the dimly lit space.

Decorated in dark red wood, she could feel the ambiance of the space and how it might welcome guests for a dinner or party. Despite the large chandelier, featuring dangling crystals on each long, spiraling arm, there wasn't much light except for the scattered wall sconces on either side of the long table. At least twenty feet in length with a glossy black top that didn't show a speck of dust, ten chairs sat on either side with more ornate captain chairs heading both ends.

It wasn't the table she found interesting.

Rather, the birch box sitting at the closest end to the dining room's entrance. She walked right up to it, actually, where it had been facing her positioned at the captain's chair.

"I was told that was for you," Mira said as she headed past Vera to continue to the connected kitchen beyond another vestibule separating the rooms at the far end. "You're welcome to open it before Vaslav gets in, yes?"

Vera didn't reply.

She couldn't look away from the birch box.

It hadn't moved, but she swore it was like staring at a foreign object. Not that it was unknown to her. She could viscerally remember the first—and last—time she had run her hands over the smooth top of the box, feeling the hinges on the back and the matching brass clasp on the front to keep it safely closed. Back then, as her father had sat beside her on her childhood bed while she traced the wood burned outline of roses entangled around a crown on the top, she had never imagined what she'd find waiting inside.

Vera still didn't touch the box.

She also didn't look away from it. The sight of it meant a lot of things but most importantly to her … it meant that her father had been there. In this house. At some point. *He* had her box; he was bringing it.

Opting to pull out the captain's chair and sit, Vera couldn't quite bring herself to reach for the keepsake meant to store a precious part of her story. A very real piece of her history that her father had taken the time and care to have preserved for her in a twelve-inch by twelve-inch box that was less than four inches deep from top to bottom.

And there it sat on a table.

Vaslav's table.

Noise echoed from the kitchen while Mira did her business, but otherwise, Vera sat alone in her thoughts and questions. Every worry tangled around another, and yet, she kept it hidden behind a veneer of a calm demeanor, and a steady gaze locked on her birch box.

Until she felt him behind her.

Vaslav hadn't even made a sound.

Not until he touched her.

Her head tipped back so she could look upward the very second his fingertips grazed the back of her neck. When she knew he was there, finding his dark stare leveling into hers, it was impossible to ignore the way his presence could fill up the space around her. The box had been only a momentary distraction to his arrival, and once he was there, she couldn't look away.

Those treacherous fingers of his, making her shiver when she should have immediately demanded to know where her father was, skipped around to the front of her throat and danced up to tap against her chin and bottom lip.

Could he feel her heart racing?

Did he know she still couldn't look away?

"Well, are you going to open it?" Vaslav asked her. "I've been dying to know what's inside since your father told me I might as well be the one to give it to you, and I'm not known for my patience."

Except, apparently, when it came to her.

2.

""I didn't expect you to come around today," Vaslav said as his fingers skimmed back down the silky soft column of Vera's throat. She swallowed against the touch, but it was the way he could feel her skin pebbling that tested his poor self-control.

"Yes, you did."

A blatant challenge.

Vera even cocked an eyebrow when she added, "You *did*."

She didn't call him out on why, and he opted not to push her into it just yet. Instead, she seemed content to let her head roll forward while his fingers ghosted over her thrumming pulse on the side of her neck before sweeping along her bare shoulder. The cable knit cashmere dress, a stone grey that complimented her porcelain flesh, left little to his imagination as he gobbled in the view of the low dip of the neckline showcasing the valleys of her breasts. With a skirt that ended just above her knees, the length was at least appropriate enough in that regard.

Everything else about it ...

Sin.

Skin-tight with looser sleeves she'd pushed up to her elbows, the very pattern accentuated her hips, and a tight waistline. A similarly low back gave him more skin to enjoy with the tips of his fingers while he let their silence stretch on even if she wasn't looking at him anymore.

"You're wearing heels again."

She had the nerve to shift her crossed legs one over the other under the table just to draw his eyes to the ankle-high suede boots with a heel slightly longer than what he would consider safe.

"Wedges," Vera all but scoffed.

"If you break your ankle walking in—"

"Don't *baby* me."

Vaslav's fingers tangled into the wispy, soft ends of her loose hair, and he tugged hard enough to hurt. Of course, it also pulled her head back so those sky-blue eyes of hers were locked firmly on him. Just the way he liked.

Even if he did find fire staring back.

"I would never," he returned, smirking only a little when he added, "We both know that's a job for your father."

A flush crept up her chest and throat at his blatant taunt, but she didn't bite the bait. Not even when he lifted his brow to make it clear he could plainly see the elephant in the room even if she wanted to pretend differently.

"Are you purposely being a prick?" Vera asked, then.

Vaslav shrugged. "I did think you were being a little

cold."

So, *yeah.*

"Well, I think you look a little tired, but you don't see me pointing it out, Vas."

That perked his amusement.

Only a bit.

"Krasavitsa, beauty, I know how I look," he said without inflection. "I have mirrors."

And dark circles, thanks to the lack of sleep over the past forty-eight hours. The tail-end of a raging migraine kept his pain at a steady, sharp five on a one-to-ten scale as well. Amongst a list of other sufferings and complaints that wouldn't make a damn difference to where this conversation was going, and none that he cared to share with her.

She didn't need to worry.

Not about him.

"But no seizures lately," Vaslav noted.

More to himself than Vera.

She still heard her.

"Oh?" Her whole face brightened.

"I'm about due for one, really."

That didn't impress Vera at all if the way her gaze narrowed, and her smile fell was any indication. "Why do you have to do that?"

"Do what?" Vaslav nodded at the birch keepsake box on the table as he came to stand beside the chair rather than behind it. She watched him the entire time. "Go on, open it. I *am* curious."

"You said my father—"

"What about him? I put him to work. He's waiting for lunch. We'll take some down for him."

Vera's pinched expression nearly made him laugh. "He's … here?"

"At the guesthouse, yes."

He enjoyed the dawning recognition lighting up her eyes, but it didn't stay long when she leveled her next questions on him. "And he's okay?"

"Why wouldn't he be?"

Dryly, Vera muttered, "You tell me."

Vaslav chuckled at that. "Stop it, *kisska*. I made a promise, didn't I? You agreed, he wasn't hurt. Simple."

Vera smacked her tongue off her top front teeth. "It was more like a deal, let's be honest."

"I don't see the difference."

"Of course, you don't."

Vera reached for the birch box with the hinged cover displaying a carefully wood-burned crown interwoven with roses. "I haven't seen this since I was sixteen."

"If it's yours, why didn't you bring it?"

"It wasn't the right time," she said.

Vaslav couldn't say he believed her, though.

She had just unlatched the brass hook on the front when he told her, "I don't appreciate uninvited visitors, and I tend to make that clear to anyone who needs the lesson more often than not, so we don't have a repeat of the mistake in the future. I'm not particularly choosy about who it is, or how it's done, Vera."

Her hands clasped the sides of the box, and she glanced sideways up at him. "He *is* okay, right?"

He didn't mind that she needed to ask again.

"Perfectly fine. The first day was the worst."

Not that he planned to explain why. Her father, on the other hand … Well, frankly, Vaslav didn't give one good goddamn what Demyan told his daughter about his arrival and treatment. If he was determined to stick around for a visit, then he would play by the rules Vaslav put in place for the time being. Including his current whereabouts.

"My mother doesn't think—"

"Ah, the *wife*," Vaslav interjected in a rumble of laughter. "Is she what sent you all the way here today?"

"You could pretend like you care."

"I do, actually. About you."

Vera blinked. "This is a strange way of showing it." *So be it.*

Vaslav gestured at the box. "Go on, then."

She flipped open the lid fast without fanfare or even hesitation. It took all of the suspense that had kept him curious about the contents of the birch box and stomped it into the ground when the lid *thunked* loudly against the table. Instead of admiring the items resting in crushed, navy-blue velvet, she glowered at him.

"They were my mother's," she said.

Vaslav reached for the larger of the two items in the box. A veil made of mostly lace that had been packaged and preserved inside a smaller, cardboard box with a plastic window for viewing. He didn't pull it out of the velvet it had been nestled into, but he studied as much of the lace's design as he could before setting it back into place.

Vera picked up the smaller box, wrapped in black leather with a hinged cover, than set aside the box preserving the veil. He guessed the contents of the box in her palm by the size alone, but she took more time to open the ring box than she had with the initial lid.

Vaslav let her.

He didn't have the same emotional attachments to things like wedding rings and other mementos. Especially when they were tied to other people. Nonetheless, when she had asked to pick her own engagement ring, he never considered it was because she already had one.

"She never got to wear the veil, but it was her grandmother's," Vera explained quietly. "The ring ... My father told me once that she sketched it out while he was clearing out the room they planned to use for my nursery. He had it made shortly after by the jeweler who made his mother's ring."

"She wore it, then? The ring?"

Vera lifted her shoulders, but even the action felt helpless when they dropped back down like a heavy weight had come to sit down on delicate bones. "Not for long."

The lid on the ring box creaked when she flipped it open. Nestled inside a similarly blue crushed velvet was an oval diamond sitting on a band of thin, white gold. At least five carats, every facet of the gem caught the dim lighting in the room. A classic style that complimented most women, but he thought was perfectly fit for Vera.

People would notice it.

The way the ring would sit on her finger; how the diamond was sized just right. It wasn't even on her finger, and already, he could practically see how she would look wearing it while she stood in a room full of people.

Like she was entirely *his*.

She took her time to reacquaint herself with the ring by tracing her thumb around the oval diamond, but she didn't pull it free from its safe place. He figured it was time to give the ring a new home. Where he intended for it to stay.

"Let me see that," he murmured.

Before she could refuse, Vaslav plucked the ring box from her hand and swallowed it with his own. He only grinned at her confused expression when he offered her his other hand to help her stand from the dining chair.

"What are you doing?" Vera asked as she allowed him to direct her a few paces away from the table.

"Something proper," he returned.

Vera laughed. "*You?*"

"You'll soon see."

And then he dropped down to one knee.

All her giggles died, then.

Vaslav gave her a rueful grin. "Cat got your tongue?"

She didn't look away as her tongue wet the pillow-soft seam of her lips, and she whispered, "That's not what you're supposed to say when you're down there with a ring."

"Right, back to the proper bit," he told her. Gone was her earlier fire, but the careful tone she had used couldn't be as easily dismissed. "Or do you not want me to ask you like this?"

Vera lifted one bare shoulder where the neckline and upper sleeve of her dress dangled dangerously. He was right about the dress, too. Every inch of the cable knit design accentuated the curves of her body in the most temping way.

"Mostly, I want you to mean it," she said.
"I'm sorry?"

"Whatever you're about to say, can you mean it?"

"Funny."

"What is?" she asked.

"Fifteen minutes ago, you thought I killed your father. Now, you want me to propose like I mean it. One thing is not like the other, Vera."

"I never thought that, actually. Or I wouldn't have come here at all."

He had no choice but to believe her. He couldn't find a reason to think she might be lying, either. More often than not, he found himself playing a dangerous game with this woman. One she didn't even realize she played, too.

A game of trust.

He blindly gave it.

She'd not yet ruined it.

How long would that last?

"Will you marry me?" Vaslav asked, holding her left hand in his while his other kept the ring box propped up in view for them both. "Because you want to. Marry me, Vera, promise me that I won't be alone ... and I'll give you the world."

He could mean that.

He *did*.

The woman had the nerve to make him squirm more when her shapely legs shifted in the wedge ankle boots a shade or two darker than her dress.

"I expect a kiss when I agree," she finally said. "If you're going to give me the illusion of a choice, then you might as well make it worth it while you're on the clock."

Vaslav's mouth twitched with a smile. "Is that a yes?"

"Am I getting a kiss?"

"*Vera*."

His sharp mutter of her name only made her laughter sweeter to his ears. It was even better when she whispered a breathy, "Fine, that's a yes."

He muffled her next burst of happy laughter with the crush of his kiss as he came up off his knee. The ring stayed safe in his hand, he couldn't even be bothered to get it in her hand first, while he kissed away the shakiness he'd felt in her hand and had heard in her words. It was bruising; he wanted to see what his roughness left behind and how well she wore it. Every unforgiving sweep of his lips captured hers until her mouth was open for him, and he could take her breath, too.

To be fair, she let him as she melted into the back-breaking squeeze of his arms to get her closer.

Vaslav pulled away from a trembling, red-lipped Vera. He tugged the ring from its spot tucked between velvet folds, still husky when he scoffed and said, "You need to stop acting like the illusion of anything I give you is a problem when you clearly like all of it, *kisska*."

The *squeak-squeak* of shoes coming to a rushed halt on the hardwood floors announced their forgotten visitor.

"Are we celebrating something?" Mira asked.

Was it because they were still close?

Could it be because they both *smiled*?

Vera's smile just happened to be a little more of a challenge. His, of course, stretched wider as the victor.

"I like it when you don't deny it," Vaslav said to Vera, too quiet for Mira to hear.

Then, to the woman waiting between the dining room and kitchen, he added, "Do you think we could find something more comfortable for Vera to wear for the ride, Mira? *Boot*-wise."

Vera's brow furrowed as she peered down at her shoes. He took her momentary distraction as a chance to slip the engagement ring on her finger. By the time she looked back up, he was able to see the surprise skip over her expression when she saw it on her finger for the first time.

"Lucky it's a perfect fit, no?" Vaslav asked. "For a family piece, I mean. I suspect he didn't have it resized."

"A ring! We *are* celebrating," Mira crowed.

The *most* excitement he had heard out of her all day. She was terribly bored without his mother sticking her fingers in every aspect of Mira's days, but he didn't regret cutting off the communication. It couldn't last long.

Vera's lips curved with her sweet happiness. "You're a trip sometimes. You know that?"

"*Mmm*," he grunted noncommittally. "Mira, the boots?"

"Yes, on it!"

He let go of Vera's hand, all too pleased with the fact that he had been right again as he reveled in the sight of her arm falling back to her side. The ring *did* snare a person's focus on her hand like a trap for the eyes. Unmistakable in the way her delicate fingers displayed it—and *him*.

His claim on her.

"Why do I need boots?" Vera asked.

"We're having lunch."

"Okay?"

He smirked. "With your father."

"I still don't see what that has anything to do with

boots."

"Soon you will."

3.

"Vera appreciated that Vaslav wasn't a liar. She did soon learn why she needed boots and exactly how he returned to the house so fast after her initial arrival. The sporty four-wheeled ROV featured a roll bar painted in neon yellow and decorative stickers of black flames on every wheel well.

Only one helmet waited in the passenger seat of the two-seater recreational off-road vehicle, and Vaslav didn't give Vera any time to argue about who would wear the helmet before he plucked it up where it waited on the black leather racing seat beyond the loose mesh that clipped to the roll bar like a makeshift door, and plunked it down on her head with a gentle *plunk* of his fist on the very top.

"Might be a little loose," he told her as his fingers spread wide on the top of the helmet to jiggle it.

Vera glowered playfully at him when he lifted the visor of the full-face shield high enough for him to see her face inside the helmet. "A little warning would have been nice."

"I don't like when people know my plans, actually."

"It's just a helmet."

Vaslav winked. "Is it?"

Vera, still holding the reasonably-sized storage cooler Mira had packed with lunch, only sighed. There wasn't much else she could do considering her hands were full. He soon took the cooler, shifting the lever handles on either end from her hands to his and shoved it to the middle block between the two seats of the side-by-side. The only spot it could go other than on her lap considering the ROV didn't even have any rear trunk space.

"Jump in," he said as he rounded the front, "and buckle up."

Vera eyed him as he went, enjoying the view of him in dark-wash denim and an old cotton sweater with lettering across the front that had long since faded. She couldn't remember a single time when he had dressed down in her presence, but he still looked good to her with every long stride of his muscled thighs.

"Will you, too?" she asked back.

"What?"

"Buckle up? I don't see a helmet for *you*. Safety first and all."

That made him laugh. A delight she wasn't expecting considering the way it lit up his scarred face. Vaslav jumped in the driver's seat of the side-by-side making it rock on the suspension from the sudden weight. "Get your priorities straight, *kisska*. Helmets and seatbelts are the very least of my problems when it comes to safety. Come on, he's been down there thirty minutes or more. I bet he's about ready to kill me for it, too."

"Kill you for what?"

"I might have left him a little busy."

Vera still didn't understand. "Are you messing with me?"

An entirely plausible scenario.

Vaslav flicked a switch on the dash and then turned the key to spark the engine to life. He had to yell over the roar of the ROV coming to life for her to hear. "Do you want to walk?"

That did the job.

Vera soon found a comfortable spot in the side-by-side's passenger seat, but she barely had time to buckle up before Vaslav yanked the shifting lever into drive and hit the gas. Her immediate reaction was to reach for the cooler to keep it steady, but she soon figured out that the way he wedged it between the seats kept it firmly in place.

Vaslav didn't speak as the ROV took the almost six acres of grass leading down to the far tree line in a mere minute at a speed that kept both passengers glued to their seats. She had noticed the dirt road that lined the trees and rounded the far edge, they even walked it together during her first visit, but they hadn't gone far enough where the metal gate closed the road from going any further beyond the bend in the tree line.

Except today.

The gate was wide open.

"Do you keep the side-by-side in the big shed with the Rolls?" Vera asked.

Vaslav didn't hear her.

Or maybe he couldn't.

Despite the windshield of clear, spotless plexiglass

in the front, the wind still whipped in through the open doors, carrying her words away with the rushing wooshes. The ROV eventually came off the grassland and hit the road, but the suspension kept the vehicle from behaving as if the sudden change in terrain affected it more than a gentle rock from grass to rocky gravel.

His focus stayed on the path ahead, and the way it curved beyond the gate, rounding the bend in the tree line. The backdrop of tall trees whizzed by in a green and brown blur with specks of reds, yellows and burnt oranges from the fall. Overhead, the fluffy clouds of white painted a blue backdrop, but she couldn't find any promise of rain in the sky.

Although she struggled to manage it, Vera was able to turn in enough time to see the very top of the Federal Colonial disappear beyond the rolling hill as they entered the midpoint of the turn in the road.

"*Look.*"

The only reason why she heard Vaslav's shout was because he let off the gas for the side-by-side. Vera swung back around in her seat as the view ahead of them began to form.

Or rather, a lake awaited to greet them.

A good three football fields in length, and at least one across, the still, dark water was framed by a mountain of climbing trees just starting to change color for the autumn season. It was a shame that a person couldn't see the sprawling, quiet lake from the main house, but as their off-road vehicle crept along the dirt road, she couldn't look away.

Like the road curving along the bend of the tree line, so did the edge of the water. It continued beyond even where she could see that the turn started to end and where a fence line of natural post stakes made of logs began. The fence, clearly a work in progress as there were no connecting lines between each log post sticking out of the ground, wasn't even stained or painted.

"Hell of a spot down here," she heard Vaslav say beside her.

Vera couldn't disagree. "The guesthouse is down here?"

"*Da.* Gets power by generator. I almost let Mira have the keys last year."

"Why didn't you?"

Vaslav tossed a grin her way. "She didn't like the walk."

Ah.

Vera didn't get the chance to respond before Vaslav pushed hard on the gas again, sending her back flat into the seat and leaving a cloud of dust from the dry road in the wake. She wasn't really paying attention to the arch of branches from trees where the road led through to a clearing because something out in the water caught her eye instead.

A black mass bobbing along the lake's surface. It took her more than a couple of blinks to discern the figure swimming slowly from one side of the lake to the other.

Marrow.

The black retriever didn't seem to be having any trouble doggy paddling his way across the lake. If anything, the dog was determined and focused.

Beyond the break in the trees where the branches swept high across the road like arches, a line of stake posts began every six feet. The unfinished fence also lined a small portion of the lake. Vera finally caught a glimpse of the front of the home Vaslav called a guesthouse where the break in the trees opened to a clearing surrounded in the colors of fall. Designed similarly on the outside to the main house, it featured gray bricks and crawling green vines that lined every long, rectangular window. Except it was like a mini version of the house on the hill. Instead of three levels, there were two, and it was barely half the size in length. She doubted it had more than two bedrooms. No towering birch trees welcomed them, and there weren't any stone steps leading to the front door, but the likeness to the main house was unmistakable all the same.

And so was the man standing by tall posts where a dirt path led from the driveway to the docks for the lake.

Her father.

Vera hadn't thought Vaslav lied to her about where Demyan was, but she didn't exactly expect to see him holding a ten-foot post at the mouth of the dock, shirtless and sweating, and glowering their way.

"See," Vaslav said over the rumble of the engine as their ROV slowed to a crawl again, "I told you he was probably getting impatient."

At the sight of the all-terrain vehicle, Demyan let go of the tall log post with one hand, and gestured wildly in their direction. For whatever reason, he glanced back at the unmoved post stuck deep in the ground, and his brow furrowed with surprise and anger.

"*You prick!*" she swore Demyan shouted.

Vaslav heard it, too.

Because he *laughed*.

Cackled, really. Like he enjoyed whatever trick he'd

successfully played on Demyan.

"All right, off you go," Vaslav told Vera then.

Her head snapped his way, and she hadn't realized until that moment how long she'd been holding her breath because it came out in a heavy *woosh*. "What?"

The side-by-side rolled to a stop in the middle of the driveway, halfway between where the road ended at the mouth and where the guesthouse waited on the other side of the drive. Vaslav yanked the shifting lever into park, and pointed at the man now coming their way. Whatever task her father had been left with by the fence was forgotten, it seemed.

"I'll take the food in and get it ready to eat on the back deck. The lake wraps around to the back of the house, too. Come in when you're ready, yeah?"

Vera blinked. "You're not leaving me alone—"

"With your father?"

He even cocked a brow at the question. She knew how silly it sounded, but his expression only drove the point home.

Her chest tightened. "I ... well," she tried lamely, still stumbling over her thoughts.

Vaslav's thin patience only extended so far with her, apparently. "Trust me, he's not even the slightest bit annoyed with you. I made sure of it. Now *go*."

Ten years.

Did he know that?

Understand it?

Vera didn't think so, but she also didn't believe that those few seconds were enough for her to explain to Vaslav that it had been a good decade since she spent more than a passing handful of minutes in her father's presence. Not by choice. *Mostly.*

Circumstances kept them apart.

Life.

Her career, too.

The few times she had been stateside for productions before her accident didn't even lead to extended stays with her parents. In a way, Vera became a woman—or stumbled into adulthood, rather—far away from the prying eyes of the people she knew loved her most. At least, when she failed, that made swallowing it easier.

Less humiliating. Even if the isolation had eaten her heart up to its last lonely shred.

At the same time, it also left her feeling like a stranger to the people she left behind. Maybe that was the problem making her nerves stay on high alert, lost connection.

Vaslav reached over to unbuckle her seatbelt, and with a single wag of his finger, she begrudgingly climbed out of the side-by-side. As she tugged off the helmet, shaking her head a bit to settle the wild strands of her hair, she could hear the approaching footsteps on the ground behind her.

She handed the helmet over.

Vaslav took it with a measured smile. "I'll see you shortly, *krasivyy.*"

"You told me the post would fall, Vaslav!"

"But only your pride took a hit, comrade," came the rueful reply.

Vaslav jerked the sporty ROV out of park and into drive once more, but he didn't step on the gas as he pulled away that time. Thankfully. Vera couldn't say she was in the mood to face her father in a cloud of dust.

Instead, she turned to find her father facing her while the backdrop of the lake painted a picture of a serene, natural beauty around his tense posturing.

"I held that for more than thirty fucking minutes," Demyan said.

Vera's brow furrowed. "Held what?"

"The post!"

She glanced at the log post in question that still stuck up straight, reaching ten feet high from where it jutted out of the ground toward the sky. Out of all the other posts, it was the only one as tall as it was, and facing a more center section of the wide lake. Another one of a similar length waited nearby on the ground.

"Did it need to be held or—"

"Apparently not!"

Vera blinked at the high pitch of annoyance coloring her father's tone of voice. "You were helping Vaslav build the fence?"

Demyan scrubbed a hand down his mouth and chin, eyeing his daughter warily but not closing the six or so feet of distance between the two. "He woke me up at five."

"In the morning?"

He nodded.

Vera squinted a bit at that. "No, thank you."

"Tell *him* that."

Um ...

Vera didn't really have to think about that option. "Another pass for me, Papa."

One didn't refuse Vaslav.

He took what he wanted.

When and how he wanted it.

Maybe it was the *papa* that did it, but Demyan's tension melted out of his strong, broad shoulders in a flash. He still didn't step toward her, but the softness in his gaze urged Vera to inch a little closer to her father.

A part of her held back, though. She kept enough space between them that he couldn't reach out and hug her just yet.

She stared into the stretch of dirt in front of them needing those few seconds to think about the things her father probably needed to hear her say. As a young girl, everyone had liked to tell her how much she looked like her dead, biological mother, Gia. That her dainty features, even her mannerisms and sprite-like demeanor was all Gia right out of bed.

Yet, Vera found familiarity most when she stared into the eyes of her father. They were the same sky-blue as hers. Cold when they were angry. Icy, even. His black hair had passed on the genetics to the mop she called her own. Maybe they weren't identical mirrors of one another, but home was still home all the same, and she felt it unquestioningly when she looked at Demyan.

A piece of it, anyway.

"It fits, I see," her father said suddenly.

His gaze had locked on the sparkling diamond sitting perfectly on her ring finger. Vera didn't even consider covering it with her other hand or hiding it behind her back to keep him from seeing a truth she bet he had already figured out by now.

"Papa, I'm engaged," Vera said, then.

She needed the words *out*.

One hurdle over.

Demyan released a heavy breath. "And without even saying a word about it to anyone, too."

What could she say to that?

Vera opted for nothing.

The pregnant pause of awkwardness didn't deter

Demyan from pushing harder.

"Do you have *anything* to say to me?"

"About this?" Vera asked, lifting her hand to show off the large diamond.

"About *anything*!"

His raised voice echoed over the quiet lake.

Vera shrugged in response. "No, not really."

Her father blinked. Whether it was from the shock of her frank answer or the situation facing him, she didn't know.

"You're always doing that to me," he murmured. "Demanding distance. Taking space. But I don't think you realize how it looks from my perspective. You don't see what I see. Every time I turn around and blink, you're someone different, Vera. *Look at you.*"

Nobody ever said Vera was perfect. Sometimes, though, she didn't recognize her own selfishness until it stared her down to the ground. Or rather, how it reflected in the eyes of her father. She never actually considered how her need to learn and express herself away from her family would hurt them.

He clapped his hands without warning, making Vera jump in place.

"You stopped holding my hand to cross the road one day, and the next you wanted to do ballet," he said. Then, Demyan clapped again. "Boom—sixteen, and you're off to Russia without as much as an argument from me because I knew you'd hate me forever if I refused you."

He clapped once more.

Vera spoke for him that time. "I'm all grown up, only talking to you on a screen, and getting married."

His hands fell to his sides, but he nodded. "It's just … a part of me thinks this is your way of running. I never could figure out what you were running away from, though. Was it me?"

"No."

Of that, she was positive.

Demyan didn't look like he believed it. "You scared me to death."

Vera let out a laugh. "*How?*"

He jerked a hand toward the guesthouse. "How, are you serious? Who is more like it!"

"You only know that because you paid someone to keep tabs on me and bring the information back, Papa."

"Which is *my* right, the *very least* I can and will do!"

To him, he was allowed his opinion, and Vera wouldn't argue the point.

What was done was done.

"You were hiding something from your mother and I," Demyan said, "and you can't fault me for finding what it was."

"No, I omitted details that weren't your business."

"You're getting married and that's not my business?" he demanded.

"The engagement is still new," she tossed back. *Weakly.*

Demyan outright scowled. With her twenty-seventh birthday approaching in only a couple of months, Vera shouldn't have folded in on herself as much as she did in the face of her father's disappointment.

You're a grown woman. Act like it, she told herself. And still …

It didn't help.

Vera opened her hands and arms in a sign of surrender. "I'm fine. I'm okay, look at me. I was going to tell you that I'd met someone. Soon," she hedged.

At that, her father's posture loosened up again. Not that it helped with the tension between them.

"It's not the state of you that worries me, Vera. It takes very little research to understand the kind of man you're involved with and let me tell you, I didn't like a lot of what I found."

"Because he's criminally affiliated, *really*?"

"Don't even start." Demyan shook his head, and eyed the house. "The *whys*. Why all of this, why *him*? Why does he do the fucking things he does? *Why*, Vera? Have you asked him any of that yet? Because when I ask why, I don't get answers. Does he at least answer to *you*?"

"I don't know what you're asking me."

"Is he forcing you—"

"I'm where I want to be," Vera said. "I've done exactly what I wanted to do, too."

It was that second when she knew it was true, too. The one thing she learned from Vaslav in their short, sporadically chaotic time together was that whatever she said, she needed to *mean* it. Especially because he wasn't a man who said things that he didn't mean. Even if they were in anger, he could apologize for it later, or a truth that would sting her from its reality.

It didn't matter.

If he said it, it was true, and he meant it.

Vera extended the same respect to Vaslav, and her promise of that only strengthened the moment she agreed to be his wife, and he slid the ring down her finger. It wouldn't matter if she did ask Vaslav the things Demyan said she should, and her questions might not even revolve around why like his had, but she didn't say that to her father.

Instead, she asked, "Could I have a hug? We can yell at each other later, you know? There's always time to fight."

And not nearly enough to catch up.

Demyan blinked. "What?"

"A hug from my father. I missed you. I can't remember the last time you hugged me, and—"

"God, yes. Come here."

That was all she needed to tell him. Demyan closed the distance separating him and his adult daughter. Time had changed a lot of things for the two of them, but the way he could make the world disappear when he wrapped her in a hug wasn't one of them.

Yes, her communication skills had been lacking. No, his worries weren't for nothing.

The hug took it all away ... at least, for a moment.

"It all happened really fast," she whispered, not knowing how else to explain the strange relationship she had stumbled into with Vaslav since their first meeting. None of it had been normal, certainly not the standard, and she couldn't say she wanted to change what she found because of it, either. Even if she wasn't ready to say what that thing she found was; how could she when she had yet to make sense of it herself?

"And I don't regret any of it," Vera added after a second.

Demyan huffed a breath into Vera's hair, squeezing her tighter when he muttered, "He's goddamn *crazy*, Vera."

"Don't say th—"

He held her away from him. Far enough that the two had to stare one another in the face as he said to her, "I can't even remember getting off my plane."

Demyan jammed a finger into his chest. "I woke up again and again only to get a rag over my face the second I was conscious. He had my associate shot in the face while he drank *tea* and told me where I would be staying like he was checking me into a hotel, Vera. Where I walked to, by the way, in the middle of the night while the bald one followed me."

Demyan scoffed. "*Follow the road. Door's unlocked.*"

She blinked at the callous way he mocked Vaslav's amusement but was more struck by how unsurprised she was at the way her father had been treated by the man. It wasn't like Demyan to just *talk* that way to her. So frankly. Hell, she was a teenager before she got him to admit he was affiliated to the mob.

Her grandfather, on the other hand ... well, Anton Avdonin never had a problem saying exactly who and what he was when asked. As long as it wasn't a cop asking the question.

"He's dangerous, likely unstable, and that's concerning to me. Whether you're willing to admit it, or not."

"He takes some getting used to," Vera tried to say.

"He woke me up with breakfast," Demyan said, "before the sun was even in the sky. With a job, he said! His mood was a hell of a lot better, mind, but given the way I was dumped on his floor, I don't particularly trust his smiles. The enemy you know is better than the one you don't."

"That's the thing, Papa."

"*What* thing?"

"You don't know him, but even if you did, that's not the point. He handles people better when he believes they don't know anything about him at all."

Demyan blinked at that, dropping his hands from

her and taking a small step back. "Vera, do you hear yourself say that, it's insane!"

"Well …" *So be it*, Vera thought. She folded her arms over her chest, and planted her booted feet, Mira managed to find a pair of hikers that fit, firmly into the ground. No doubt, the sight of her, the contrast between her dress and footwear, and the entire scene was silly to Demyan. She wished she cared. "Nobody said you had to like it. *You* came here."

She expected anger.

Maybe it was even justified.

After a pause that made Demyan look frozen in time against the soft movement of the lake and breeze in the trees, he barked out a laugh.

"Oh, God," he crowed.

Vera shifted a bit on her heels. "Why are you laughing?"

It took another low rumble of laughter before Demyan managed to mumble his reply, "That's what he told me, too."

"I mean …" She let her palms helplessly slap against her thighs over the cashmere dress. "It's true."

"Was that a cooler I saw on the ROV?" Demyan asked, then.

The change of subject brought Vera sweet relief. "Yeah. Salad, bread, coffee. Something sweet, too."

"Is he going to give me back the rest of my things, too?"

Vera hesitated long enough for her father to roll her eyes. Defensively, she said, "I didn't know he'd taken your things."

"And my phone!"

"I'll get your phone back," Vera snapped. "Did you

even bother to ask for it yourself?"

"I asked enough questions to learn he didn't like to be asked questions, Vera."

Fair enough.

There was one thing she could fix.

Vera pulled her phone from the pocket of her dress, one of the best features next to the neckline, in her opinion, and offered it to her father. "Here. Call Ma. She's very worried."

She didn't need to say it twice.

Demyan took the phone and grumbled, "Yeah, I bet."

4.

I'm where I want to be.

Vaslav was left to ponder those words while he should have been enjoying the Olivier salad and sourdough rye bread Mira had made to go with the dark roasted coffee to wash the dense food down. Instead, he'd made it halfway through his lunch as Vera's conversation trailed on with her father and Vaslav made no effort to engage.

He didn't care to talk.

He'd rather *think*.

Obviously, the food he promised to get ready on the rear porch didn't even get unpacked. He'd been too busy eavesdropping on the terse, and sometimes loud, conversation between Demyan and his daughter. Not that Vera mentioned that when she finally came through the front doors to find he'd left it sitting on the dining room table inside the house.

They did get the food to the back, though.

At least, while he watched the lake nobody seemed

to care if he wasn't involved and engaged with their discussion.

"December first, I think," Vera said, drawing Vaslav from his pensive thoughts.

Only because Demyan said, "Your birthday?"

"My birthday," she agreed.

"For what?"

Vaslav's sudden emergence into the conversation between a father and daughter, not caring who he interrupted, earned him an annoyed glance from Demyan. Vera, on the other hand, only peered up at him with sweetness. It curved her lips into an indulgent smile and brightened her eyes.

"You were spacey for a minute. I didn't even think you were listening."

"Hmm." Vaslav nodded at the lake, and lifted a hand from the table to point at the speck of black emerging from the thick bush on the other side of the shallow end of the lake closest to the porch. "I was keeping an eye on Marrow."

The dog made a loud splash when he jumped in. The only other noise but for the birds in the trees that would soon be leaving for the winter and the hum of the generator at the far end of the house keeping all the decorative lights that hung overhead stay lit. In the shade of the tall oaks, it allowed the porch a bit of light in the daytime.

At the other side of the table, Demyan made an anxious noise. "If that fucking dog comes near this porch, I'm going in the house."

Vaslav didn't hide his chuckle. "Ah, he was only a little bothered about you last night. Give it a rest."

"And what about this morning?" Demyan demanded.

Well …

Vaslav considered the aggressive behavior the dog displayed while observing the two men pounding in stakes that morning for the fence line. Marrow barked for a solid half hour before finally slinking away to jump in the lake, clearly disturbed by his master's new companion. Nonetheless, during that half hour of non-stop barking, if Demyan even looked the dog in the eye, Marrow started creeping forward in preparation for attack, teeth bared.

"He doesn't like guests," Vaslav said with a shrug. Then, he tossed a tight-lipped smile Demyan's way, adding, "Or men."

"Can't imagine where he picks up that attitude."

Vera laughed into her hand but quickly hid her amusement in a bite of sourdough bread. He enjoyed the way her blush crept up her throat the longer his piercing stare lingered on her. *Does she feel the way she tests every ounce of self-control I have just by being near?*

He could kiss her giggles quiet. Or he could even enjoy the way she'd fluster and push back against him if he felt like correcting her behavior when men of certain status sat down at a table together. Both would end in a way *he* liked … eventually. Whether it was angry or not. Vas got off either way.

Vaslav couldn't say that for the other two people at the table.

Damn it all to hell.

Vaslav raised his brow and observed Marrow paddle closer in their direction. Every few paddles followed a loud bark that echoed over the lake, and snapped back across the property straight into Vaslav's brain. "A breed thing, I think." Whistling high, he called to the pup, "Get a stick to toss, you shit. Don't come over here with that bark of yours again. You're making my head pound on a *good* day, Marrow."

"Right, a breed thing," Demyan muttered. "That's what's some shit, right there."

Another rough laugh escaped Vaslav, although at least he did try to hold it in. "I can hear the Brooklyn in you there a bit. It's been a while since I've been around to that side of the world, let me say."

"Adrik sends his regards from Jersey."

"What did he have to say about your trip here when you told him your plans?" Vaslav asked.

An honest curiosity. Adrik Vasin, whose son Koldan had taken over his organization a while back, was one of the few vory in America that Vaslav would sit down to do business with should the need arise. Mostly because men like Adrik had started their life in the brotherhood in their motherland, and still paid respects to where they came from.

He appreciated loyalty.

Even if it did come in the form of a three-percent cut off the top of a multi-billion dollar smuggling and trafficking organization. Cocaine and weapons, for the most part. Not that it mattered. The monetary value made the difference.

"Well?" Vaslav asked after a noticeable pause from the man across the table.

Demyan, distracted by the way Vera smiled at the paddling dog who actually was searching for a floating stick in the lake, glanced his way. "He didn't tell me anything. My father, on the other hand ... all they have to do at their age is *talk*. He told Anton I had a death wish. The message got passed along."

"But apparently," he mused, "not heard."

Demyan wisely chose to be quiet.

Peering down at Vera again where she sat at the outdoor dining table next to him, Vaslav asked, "And what about December first, yeah? I didn't forget."

She finally took her gaze away from the dog in the water who had, in fact, found a stick. He really needed to join the pup down here more. It was Marrow's favorite spot.

For obvious reasons.

"I thought it would be a good date," Vera told him.

"Yes, but for *what*?"

She gestured at her father. "He asked if I'd picked one for the wedding."

Ah.

There was the missing piece; the one bit of missing information from the initial conversation he hadn't been properly engaging at the table.

His surprised hum had Vera's brow lifting higher before she popped a piece of sliced pickle into her mouth, and then sucked the juice from the tip of her thumb. The staple at any Russian's meal, the pickle gave her something to chew around her barely suppressed grin.

She put him on the spot.

Knew she'd done it.

And liked it.

Cheeky witch.

Vaslav's gaze narrowed slightly at her challenge.

He considered asking her right then and there where she planned on sleeping that night. He had an opinion on the matter, of course, but did she want to discuss it right now?

"Vera," he warned.

The tone should have done it.

A dainty shrug fell from her bare shoulder where the neckline of her dress draped down to expose everything from her collarbone to her shoulder blade. "Yeah. It'll be my birthday and our anniversary on the same day."

Vera's gaze drifted her father's way when Demyan said, "I hear a common complaint between wives and their husbands is the man being forgetful of certain times of the year. Like important dates. Could be useful."

Vaslav stiffened, turning to ice in an instant. The switch that flipped on in his brain went from zero to sixty instantly. It would have been nothing, *meant* nothing, for him to reach across the table in that moment to get a better grip on Demyan's head to smash it through the pristine glass beneath their plates.

He didn't know where the self-control came from that held Vaslav back from giving into the sudden, intrusive violent urges toward his unwanted and resentful guest, but it may have been the fact that being near Vera made him … happy.

Or something like it.

Content, at least.

It just wasn't enough to stop him from wanting to kill her father.

He didn't know if the other two people at the table noticed the sudden change in his demeanor. Frankly, he didn't give either of them the time to before he'd stood up from the table with enough abruptness to make Vera jump beside him. Her shocked, widening stare followed him as he scrubbed a hand down his thicker, but not by much, growth of facial hair on his throat, and walked away from the lunch without a single glance back.

Utensils clattered at his departure.

"Vas?" Vera called. "Where are you going?"

It was only a few strides from the table before he slid through the sliding glass doors leading into the rear rooms of the guesthouse's ground level.

"What happened?" Demyan asked, his voice fainter with every step Vaslav took further away.

"I don't know," he heard Vera say. "Just … give me a second, Papa."

Chair legs scraped against the deck wood.

Vaslav kept walking even when she called his name again. He needed a second, too.

Or perhaps more than a few.

By the time Vera had caught up to him, he'd paced a line in the dirt at the front of the house and finally settled on jumping into the driver's seat of the side-by-side. Vera came to stand just beyond the opening from door with her arms folded over her chest. He considered not even giving her an explanation, to let the dust from the ROV's tires say his goodbye.

The knot of confused sadness between her eyes when she tipped her head to the side stopped him from turning the engine over. The loosely tied laces of the hiking boots on her feet spoke to how hastily she'd pulled them on trying to get out of the house.

"What are you doing?" Vera asked. "I thought we were having lunch?"

Jaw tight, he shook his head once and forced out a clipped, "No."

"What happened? Something just happened, right?"

"Are you staying?" he asked.

Vera blinked. "What?"

"Your father will not be leaving this property unless it is to leave the country. So, if you have any plans to stay with him for an extended visit, let me know now. I'll have your things brought from the city."

"*Vaslav.*"

Her quiet exclamation of his name only irritated him further.

It wasn't even her damn fault.

"How am I going to get back to the house?" she asked then.

"*Walk.*"

It wasn't *that* far. Especially in her current footwear with decent ankle support.

"But tie up those goddamn laces if you get any bright plans," he said for her benefit.

Vera's brow jumped high when he turned the key forward, and the engine of the side-by-side roared to life. Over the growl, she yelled, "You can bring my things!"

He glanced her way.

Vera, even scowling at him, was terribly beautiful in front of a backdrop of gray bricks and green vinery. "I *would* like to spend time with my father as long as you don't intend to make it a hassle the entire damn time."

Fair enough.

He nodded once.

Vera's defensive stance loosened as her arms fell to her sides. "I just don't understand ... *you* brought me down to have lunch, we were only talking, Vas. This is my father, who by the way, I *know* you're aware how long it's been since I've spent meaningful time with him, so can't you just—"

"That's the only reason he's even alive."

Her lips flattened into a grim line. "He didn't *do* anything!"

"He's *here*."

"You brought him here!" she shouted.

A second time.

Despite his calm tone.

"No, he *came* here," Vaslav corrected, "knowing you were involved in some way with me and expecting at the same time that I wouldn't intend to have words with him in the meantime. *Foolishness.* A stupid thought for a man like him. Or maybe he loves you too much to think about the nuances of a man in *my* position."

"Maybe that's what it is," she said.

His confusion tightened his shoulders. "I don't—"

"Your position. The *real*, and proverbial. I don't have a clue about any of it." She waved two dainty hands his way and added, "What I see is what I get with you. You keep expecting me to put the rest of the puzzle together but apparently, I also have to make the pieces."

"You'll run," he said.

Vera's head shook gently. "What does that even mean?"

"Everything you think you want to know … once you do, you're gone. And then I'll have to chase you, *kisska*. You won't give me a choice, and as you like to point out, I've already taken quite a few of those away from you. What's really left? How rose-tinted would you like your life to be from here on out, or should I just drop the pretense altogether?"

"Go to hell," she muttered weakly.

Vaslav laughed, cold and uncaring when he focused

his attention back on the wheel of the side-by-side. "You think I'm not a monster beneath the smile you're so fond of; you think I won't hurt you because you crave my touch. You have no idea how wrong you are. Vera, I won't even say sorry."

"You don't know that," she called over the metal clang of him roughly shifting the side-by-side into gear. "You don't know what I'll do; you don't even know if I love you, and I bet that's what scares you, too. I thought you didn't like to be called a coward? So why are you being one?"

His foot slammed hard into the brake before the bike could roll more than a few inches forward, and his head snapped to the side. "*Kisska—*"

The front door slammed shut.

He didn't even see her go inside.

You silly woman, he thought.

She didn't fully comprehend what she had just asked for; her unintended challenge met its mark like an arrow straight through the heart. A love like his would absolutely ruin her.

Vaslav shot one last glance at the front door before he hit the gas. *Well, then—game on, Vera.*

*

The following chilly, damp night found Vaslav reclining in one of the wicker chairs as the sun started to set beyond the trees. Not with the rest of the set in front of the outdoor fire pit, but rather, further down on the hill where the taller grass swayed at his knees when he stood.

Halfway between the house and the tree line.

Almost nowhere.

It felt like it when he was drunk, anyway.

The tip of his finger toyed with the rim of the mostly empty bottle of vodka where it rested between the legs of the chair. It wouldn't be long before he couldn't stand to sit outside in nothing more than a thick sweater and denim. He might as well take advantage of the good weather. Or rather, what remained of it.

With eighty proof swimming thick in his veins, he could almost be lulled into a comfortable nap with his neck resting on the curved back of the chair, and each of his legs stretched out in cool, tall grass. If it weren't for the familiar growl of an engine …

Sighing when he heard tires rolled to a stop on nearby gravel, Vaslav instantly regretted not downing what remained of the almost two liters of vodka when he still had the chance. That time ran out the second his newly appointed *nurse*, Igor did not think that joke was funny, knew Vaslav had access to the liquor.

"Where did you get the vodka? Did you hide that from me?" Igor demanded, his every word punctuated by a stomped foot through the grass.

Vaslav didn't dignify Igor's question with a response, but he did straighten up a little more in the chair. Just in enough time to watch the man yank the bottle up from the ground. Then, he promptly tipped it over and dumped the two or three mouthfuls that remained onto the ground at his feet.

"*Waste* of good vodka," Vaslav cursed at his friend. "I should kill you—"

Igor let out a hard exhale, and his stare nailed into a suddenly still Vaslav in the chair. "Do you want the fucking seizures to stop, or not?"

"Right now, it'd just be good if the sky would stop

swirling." Vaslav glanced down, muttering, "And the ground, too."

Igor spat a Russian curse and whipped the bottle to the ground. The thick glass didn't even crack, and even bounced a little before coming to a stop at Vaslav's feet.

"No alcohol, *no* Vicodin, you know this!"

"But I didn't agree," Vaslav replied through a grinding jaw.

He *half* agreed, to be frank. Hence the molar pain from his sore jaw because he'd been twenty-four hours since his last dose of an opioid narcotic, and of any pill, actually. He couldn't say as much for the liquor, but that wasn't because he'd been *craving* vodka.

Vaslav simply wanted to *sleep*.

It wasn't asking much, but if he couldn't take his regular cocktail of medication to get through a day and night, then living was a second-by-second battle for survival at times. Like now.

Who would have known that mixing nearly a liter of vodka a day with a handful of pills meant to either help his head, his gut, or his sleep wasn't exactly *great* for his health? Once Igor learned Vaslav had been in contact with the doctor responsible for the newest file on his desk, the one full of reports on brain scans and imagery, he didn't waste time getting on the phone.

To the doctor in question, that was.

Vaslav wasn't interested in being the guinea pig for anyone's game of Ring Around the Medications, but a conversation with the doctor over the phone, while Igor listened in, at least convinced him of one thing.

The seizures were likely his own doing.

Accidentally, of course, as Doctor Bogdan Nikitin

had opted to carefully explain to Vaslav. He couldn't just *mix* pills to his liking even if he did have ready access and it seemed to make things better for a short time. Add liquor into his cocktail, and blood toxicity was a real possibility. The man offered to do bloodwork to confirm, which Igor said Vaslav should do, but he refused.

He'd go clean first.

No pills.

No mixing.

Less stress could help too, the doctor had said just before Vaslav ended the conversation without a proper goodbye.

He'd barely wanted to make the phone call, let alone get an entire list of orders he was required to follow that would do nothing to make his days bearable.

Bullshit.

Every bit of it.

Unless it worked, he mused.

Vaslav chuckled at his inner thoughts, and the action wasn't missed by Igor who shot him a curious, but not amused, glance.

"Did you really have to guzzle it while I was down the hill?" he asked Vaslav.

He shrugged. "You would have tried to take it from me."

"You sound like a child."

Vaslav chuffed. "You're entitled to your wrong opinion."

"*Vas.*"

Ugh.

"I need to sleep tonight," he said. "Give it twenty minutes, and the vodka will finish me right off."

"Try a hot shower. I'll even help you back to the house."

"While a knife stabs through your eyeball?" Vaslav shot back. "That's going to be a hard task for you."

"Knock it off."

"Ah." He waved Igor off. "I let you clean out the house of any pills."

"I thought liquor, too."

Vaslav squinted at that. "I need something."

And it couldn't be a half of a pack of sleeping tablets, according to that prick in the city. Not on top of everything else.

"At least tonight—Christ, it's only been a *day*," Vaslav added.

Not even a good day, for that matter. If he were an honest man, Vaslav might admit that having Vera as close as he did, but not within the four walls of his own home, did not help the matter of his mood or the constant churning in his gut.

"You're going to kill yourself," Igor said.

Vaslav let out a heavy breath. "Maybe, yeah."

"You don't have to speed it up, no?"

The morbid joke landed perfectly for a tipsy Vaslav who knew better than to down nearly two liters of vodka within the time span it would take his man to drive the ROV down to the guesthouse and power off the generator system for the evening. That didn't mean he intended on telling Igor he was right, though.

"Are they fighting, do you think?" he asked without warning.

Igor seemed to know who he meant without the explanation. "Wouldn't you know better than me? I found you pounding in fence posts with the man this morning again."

Vaslav rolled his eyes, refusing to admit that the entire time he was down the hill earlier in the day, Vera had all but refused to speak to him. Clearly, she still had feelings about their discussion the day before. "That's the only thing I like about him; he's willing to do a job with me."

"I offered to do that job with you," Igor pointed out.

"*You* talk while we do it. And you didn't answer me. Are they getting along?"

Igor sucked on his two front teeth, muttering, "I'm not sure. He's not that interested in having a conversation with me whenever I'm around. I don't take offense. Her father isn't exactly here to chat with me, is he?"

Vas tipped his head to the side in silent agreement, but then he replied, "He also doesn't have a choice but to be where he is."

Neither did she, in a way.

Igor passed Vaslav a wary glance. "Kiril still doesn't believe you won't cut off his dick for going into Vera's place last night to pack a weekend bag."

"He does understand that it would have been already done, yes?" Vaslav asked back. "*I* told him to do it. I got on the phone myself."

The other man only shrugged.

"Explains why he's been missing all day," Vaslav said to himself.

"Yeah, well … You know you're going to puke all that vodka up, yeah?" Igor asked, his concerned tone warring with his disgust.

Yes.

Yes, he did. Vaslav could already feel it sloshing

because he'd taken that forty-percent way too fast for his stomach and liver. Yes, he'd puke until he couldn't anymore.

And then he would feel like absolute death.

"But I'll sleep," Vaslav mumbled.

Like a fucking rock.

That's what mattered.

5.

Dewy blades of grass kissed Vera's calves as she walked along the side of the lake. The rhythmic *plunk, plunk, plunk* of a sledgehammer banging a fence stake into the ground greeted her before even her father did. Demyan, fully focused on his task, didn't notice Vera until she was standing just a few feet away.

He tossed the tool in his hand, hammer down, against his most recent post. Over the course of only a couple of days, the fence line of natural wood posts had started to take form along the edge of the lake. They had the entire line of the lake, a good two hundred feet around the house, finished with single standing posts. What good the fence would do to keep someone out of the lake, should it need to, she didn't know. It did, however, give the landscape a homey, country appeal. She couldn't deny that.

"Where's your friend this morning?" she asked her father.

"Who'd know?" he muttered back.

She didn't press the issue.

The morning before, Vera hadn't even bothered to make her way out to speak to Vaslav when he came riding down on the ROV. If the man couldn't at least *talk* out his issues, then she wouldn't waste time trying to pry the details from him.

Besides, what was different?

Vaslav had been mean before.

This hadn't even hurt.

It was more than a little amusing to see Demyan wipe the sweat from his brow with the back of his silk sleeve. What he came with, he had, apparently. Nothing more, and nothing less. He didn't exactly pack the type of clothing he'd need to do hard labor, like pounding in fence posts from five until eight in the morning, but that didn't exactly stop him, either.

Even in slacks, that desperately needed an iron, and a silk button down that would likely soon find a garbage can, Demyan found something to do.

Resting his arms over the top of the fence post, Demyan squinted one eye at his daughter where she stood in her borrowed hiking boots, wrapped tightly in an over-sized cardigan that Kiril had provided along with a bag of other clothes. "You're up early."

"Is it?"

"Barely seven," her father replied.

Vera nodded, accepting his account of the time for what it was, but not able to confirm it other than the early chirp of birds in the trees and the cold mist clinging to the top of the lake's surface. Given the sun wasn't even high enough in the sky to warm the air, though, she knew he wasn't lying.

"Someone should be running down breakfast soon, then," she said. Thankfully, Demyan had learned how to run the generator system so she woke up to power and running water unlike the morning before. "Did you meet Mira yet, *properly*?"

"The first night. I wasn't entirely right, to be fair, so there's not much to tell."

Vera chewed on her bottom lip, mumbling, "Oh."

"Didn't seem like much of a talker."

"She's … it takes a bit, and she's very loyal to Vaslav so if he's even the slightest bit uncomfortable, then she usually is, too. Like most everyone else around him," Vera added.

Although, she instantly regretted giving away as much information about Vaslav's moods and how it affected the people in his life. Just because she noticed those sorts of things didn't mean that he would want Vera sharing them.

"But that's not important," she told her father quickly.

Demyan shrugged. "I suppose."

The borderline safe conversation didn't exactly leave Vera feeling fulfilled, but it wasn't anything new between the two.

"Are you ever going to come back home?" Demyan asked.

She hadn't been ready for it.

Vera stumbled over a weak deflection. "I mean, when did I really have time … not to mention, it's not like right *now* is a great time to plan something like that."

"I didn't ask why."

Yeah.

God.

Vera stopped avoiding her father's gaze, and settled on telling him the truth. "It never really felt like home, Papa. I was so focused on being something that I didn't really learn to enjoy where I was and what I had."

"You're saying you didn't have anything to miss? You don't miss us … do you not want us?"

She flinched. "It's not like that."

"It sounds like that."

Her heavy sigh quieted Demyan from saying anything more.

She was also *busy*.

Not that Vera wanted to repeat that excuse to her father, but it was still true. From the time she was sixteen until the day she was forced to retire from being a professional ballerina, she didn't stop. Ballet had taken nearly every second of her life, and what time she did have to grow and be a person of her own making, she hadn't wasted it flying between countries because there were people she left behind who missed her.

Was it selfish?

Fine.

She didn't regret it.

"I grew up and learned a lot about who I was and wanted to be because I wasn't at home," Vera said. "I had a different kind of influence shaping my perspective. And that's not a bad thing, but it didn't have anything to do with you, or Claire … anybody, really."

"Before or after your injury?" Demyan shot back.

"That's not fair," Vera whispered, blinking back the sudden sting of tears welling in her eyes, "you don't know what that was like for me. Especially after it happened. To be—"

"You didn't let us, either."

"Wasn't it bad enough for me to be a failure to myself? Why did I have to go home to be one, too?" she asked, every word getting progressively higher and shriller.

She didn't want to yell, or argue, or do any of this at all.

"You know what, I already told you what matters here, I'm where I want to be," Vera said, and the declaration loosened her father's tight shoulders. "Do we really have to do this?"

"Just because you can make choices doesn't mean I have to like them."

"But you don't get a say in them, either, Papa."

Demyan nodded once, and then waved a hand at the quiet scenery around them. "Yeah, tell me about it."

"What's that supposed to mean?"

"Can't say I had any choice once I got here, can we?" he asked.

"To be fair, neither did I."

"The bigger issue with that is how you don't seem to have a problem with it," Demyan pointed out.

Vera lifted an eyebrow high. "Maybe that's because a part of me likes it."

"*Vera.*"

"And him," she added, ignoring her father's warning. "I also like him." *A lot*, she thought. "So maybe if you have something to say about that, now's the time to do it and move on with it."

"Would you even hear me say it? Would you let me, as your father, say it?"

Did he want honesty?

Vera gave it, anyway. "I didn't ask *you* to love him, you're not the one who has to."

Demyan didn't push the line she drew in the sand with that statement, instead asking, "But do you? Do you love him?"

She refused to drop her father's piercing stare when she replied only, "And I didn't say you had to like him, either."

Demyan shook his head and failed to suppress a frustrated grin that he eventually scrubbed away with the palm of his hand. "*God*, you're your mother all over. Stubborn like nothing. Roman's gonna give me a stroke before he's thirty but *you*—"

"Was she like me?" Vera asked, then.

That stopped her father right up.

Demyan tipped his chin a bit higher as he eyed Vera and the way she hugged her oversized cardigan close to keep the cold away from her bare legs and arms. She hadn't bothered to change out of the tank top and cotton shorts she wore to bed.

He nodded at her instead of answering the question, and said, "Why don't you get in the house? I managed to keep the fireplace going last night. You don't need to be out here."

She didn't move. "I meant Gia, not Claire."

Demyan swallowed audibly while his lips pressed together, and he stared out at the lake. Anywhere but at Vera for more than a handful of seconds. "Yeah, I know," he said, emotion thick in his hoarse voice. "Frankly, she never liked to listen to me, either, Vera."

Huh.

"Your brother bet me a thousand dollars I wouldn't be able to even get a vacation out of you."

Vera's brow dipped. "A vacation?"

"Like a date and time. Even a plan, Vera." Demyan

64

rolled his eyes and slapped a hand against the top of the post as he pushed away from it. "I should have shut my mouth; Roman likes taking my money too much. He gets a complex from it."

"In the spring," she said suddenly.

Demyan's head snapped up at that. "For what?"

"I'll come home to visit in the spring."

That declaration only had her father staring toward the arch of overhanging trees where the dirt road entered the drive of the private guesthouse. Without saying anything at all, his gaze said it all. *Says who?*

"Maybe I can convince Vaslav to take a late honeymoon to the states," Vera said.

Not *seriously*.

Demyan barked out a laugh. "Right, I'll believe that one when I see it. From what I hear, that man doesn't leave this country unless he has no other choice. People watch, see ... he's known for making it very hard for anyone to find him in the first damn place. If you think he'll be seen within fifty miles of me, you're not as smart as I gave you credit for." Gesturing at their surroundings, he added, "Why do you think he's put me in a little bubble where only *he* knows I exist for the moment? It's not even personal. He just doesn't do business that way. And a ring on your finger won't change any of that, I promise you."

The news didn't shock her.

His account of it, however, did.

"Men in familiar circles, right?" she asked, knowing her father would understand perfectly fine. Of course, he'd have an intimate look at Vaslav Pashkov, the international criminal. Birds of a feather flocked together. Wasn't that how the saying went?

Demyan openly frowned. "I never hid the things I

did from you. I didn't pretend to be a different man from who I was. Can he say the same? Do you even know what bed the beast is making for you?"

She hated that he was right.

And that it still didn't make a difference.

"What does it matter about the bed," she returned, wanting this to be the last time she had this conversation with her father, "as long as he's in it with me?"

*

It was closing in on lunchtime before Vera finally learned the truth about Vaslav's lack of appearance that morning. She didn't pretend to be pleased about the sight that greeted her inside the man's master bathroom, either.

Clearly hungover, besides his grey pallor, the dark circles under his eyes gave away his ill feelings and exhaustion, Vaslav reclined in a free-standing bathtub of steaming hot water. With his eyes closed, he didn't notice her approach. At least, that's how it seemed.

Steam clung to the air.

No bubbles or oils offered any scent. There wasn't even a candle lit on the counter, so she had to flick the lights on herself.

Not that he liked that.

The water sloshed violently as he jerked to awareness. Vera didn't move from her spot in the doorway while Vaslav blinked away his confusion and settled on her figure across the room.

"Mira told me you got drunk last night," she said.

"*Mira* has a big fucking mouth," he grumbled as he settled back into the tub with his arms falling limp over the outer edges.

"Any reason you felt like you needed to drink two liters—"

"It wasn't the entire bottle. And if you don't mind, when you bitch your voice feels like someone is hammering nails into my goddamn ears." He squeezed his eyes shut again, but she could see the lines of tension on his forehead that spoke of pain. "*Shut up.*"

Vera sucked in a sharp breath at his viciousness. "The migraines are back?"

"The migraines don't *stop.*"

Right, right.

Vera had to remember that.

She quickly flipped the lights back off, but opted not to move from the doorway of the bathroom. "I didn't walk up, by the way. Igor gave me a ride when he came down to check on things at noon."

"*Hmm.*"

"I was serious about the date, Vas."

That cracked his eyes back open. "What?"

He didn't look at her, but rather, focused on the wall of tiles at the foot end of the tub. At least with his attention partially distracted from her, Vera didn't feel like it was such a dangerous thing to let her own gaze wander over the man. From his damp, tattooed chest to the strong line of his shoulders covering the rounded run of the head of the tub. Even his muscular thighs dusted with dark hair, both visible as he sat with his knees bent above the water, dragged her focus in and twisted her thoughts with the thread of lust.

If he asked her to, she'd join him. Hell, if he said the right words, she'd probably crawl across the floor naked just to get inside that tub with him. It wasn't even sex that called her to him. Something else entirely curled around her waist like an invisible rope, tightening and tugging, though she pretended like she didn't feel it.

No doubt, he'd make the world disappear.

And she'd like it.

It didn't take Vaslav long to realize she hadn't answered him. He caught her staring, and she couldn't even be bothered to pretend as if she was ashamed.

He wagged a finger her way, asking, "What's all that for?"

"What?"

"You know, that *look*."

Vera preened the shorter strands of hair framing her face as a way to avoid what he said. "Are we talking about the date for the wedding or—"

"Your birthday. The first. December. I know it."

"Yes, but do you like it?"

"It's soon enough," he returned. "It works."

Less than two months.

It didn't leave a lot of time for planning.

Not that she cared.

Vera nodded. "Okay. I'll just …" She gestured toward him and the tub; his bath, really. "I'll let you get some rest. My father finished the posts along the side of the lake that faces the house, by the way, if you're feeling up to coming down to check it out later."

"This morning?"

"Yeah."

She didn't miss the telltale curve of a possible smile on Vaslav's face at the news, but as fast as it was there, it left. Like it hadn't been there to begin with.

"Huh," he eventually grunted.

Settling back into the tub with closed eyes, and a slightly more relaxed expression, Vaslav pulled in a deep breath and released it in a slow exhale. Vera gave him a few more seconds before she turned to leave. Mira had come down with Igor to bring lunch, and despite the argument the two put up when she learned of Vaslav's escapade with vodka the night before, Vera ended up winning the battle.

Hence why she stood there.

"It helped me to sleep," she heard him say.

Vera didn't turn around. "Drinking like a fool?"

"Like a *drunk*."

Good God.

She wished that disgusted her, if anything, it just hurt. It killed her to think that to ease his suffering in one way, he needed to find a different kind of hell.

"And Vera?"

She glanced back at him to find he had opened his eyes again, and watched her studiously. "Yeah, Vas?"

"December first is perfectly fine. Tell your father we'll send an invitation."

He couldn't know it, she didn't plan to share, but the news offered her a little relief. Given the way Vaslav behaved now with her father, she couldn't imagine that he'd willingly invite Demyan back to the country. Even if it was for Vera's wedding.

"And just how many of those will there be?" Vera arched her eyebrow, adding, "Invitations, I mean."

"Less than you think."

"Give me an idea."

"Count them on two hands."

Vera's eyes widened. "Ten?"

"Minus me, you, Igor, and Mira," he returned. "So, six."

"Six!" His amused, dark chuckles had her spinning around on the spot. "You can't be serious! That leaves three guests after my mother, father, and Hannah."

"Don't you have a brother?" Vaslav asked, sounding honestly curious. "Won't he want to come?"

"I don't even think he's allowed to leave the country."

Roman Avdonin's legal issues had followed him since he was a young teen. Vera didn't act like she understood the demons chasing her brother to seek out wild things.

"Two guests left, I suppose," Vaslav said, pointing a finger her way. "You can't forget Kiril. I bet you could convince him to be your flower boy."

His attempt to humor her didn't distract Vera from the main point at hand. "So basically, nobody."

Not *nobody*, nobody. The important people to her would be there, and that counted for something. It still wouldn't be a terribly big event, clearly. That helped with the planning aspect, anyway. It wasn't exactly how she imagined her wedding day, but then again, the man sitting in a tub fifteen feet away wasn't the knight in shining armor that the world promised little girls, either.

Maybe this was better.

He tipped his chin up and watched her like he was an eagle soaring high that had just landed sights on its prey. "Well, nobody but me and you."

She shivered.

His voice alone could do it.

"And you like that, don't you?" she asked.
Vaslav smiled. "Me and you?"
She nodded.
"Oh, *kisska*, you know I do."

6.

"What are you doing in my den?"

Not even the anger heating Vaslav's tone could make Vera move from where she sat. The piles of papers in her hand were just too heavy; they kept her locked in place, glued to the plush leather office chair she'd once been mesmerized by when she found him sitting there, too. Staring down with an unseeing gaze she couldn't really look away from what she'd discovered on his desk, but the words she'd read on the paper no longer made sense.

Or maybe …

It made *too much* sense.

And it hurt.

"I said, *what* are you doing in here?" Vaslav demanded.

His footsteps padded one after another on the hardwood floor. Closer to her, but she still didn't move an inch. He'd used the stairwell attached to the master suite upstairs to come down. She'd only noticed the hidden door at the far end of the walk-in closet by total accident. A few dirty items of laundry caught her attention in the bedroom, and so she'd opted to pick it up and take it to the basket she knew was in the closet for Vas even though she was well aware that Mira had a job to do.

That information just happened to be one of the first rules made clear to Vera on her first trip to the house while they were walking the property.

"Vera, I know good and well you're not deaf—"

"I only meant to tidy up the den," she said, stopping his next words from stabbing into her like the first had. He could be so careless with the way he said things; unwilling to bend even if it meant breaking her in the process. Words hurt, too. "Like I did in the bedroom."

Which was clearly the wrong thing to do.

It must not have taken Vaslav long to realize Vera didn't leave right after their conversation in the bathroom as he came to a stop in front of the desk with only a bath towel wrapped around his waist. He hadn't even taken the time to dry his hair; his trembling shook the water droplets down from each dark strand to his shoulders.

Igor hadn't given her a time frame, and she wasn't scared to make the walk back to the guesthouse, anyway. It wasn't that much more of a walk than the one she'd make almost daily to The Swan House not too long ago.

"I know I told you not to go snooping more than a cursory walk around," Vaslav said.

Not with as much anger, though.

He'd noticed what she held.

"I didn't *snoop*," she returned hotly. "I picked up a

few things because even though you *have* Mira to do that, it doesn't look like she has lately."

At least, not in the bedroom and master suites.

Or the den.

Vaslav didn't dignify her statement with a response.

"Give me that folder," he demanded.

Even his voice shook.

Vera held the papers, and the legal sized folder that the messy stack had been scattered over. "I wasn't *looking* for it." She pointed at the desk and ignored the way her hand trembled. "It was right there. Out in the open."

"In *my* den. My locked den," he said, a desperation clinging to the edges of his words. "Give it to me."

"No."

"Vera," he said, stepping closer and using one hand to brace himself on the edge of the desk as he leaned over to attempt a swipe at the papers. She only needed to lean a couple of inches sideways in the chair to be far enough out of his reach. That earned her a cuss, and his fist slamming down on the desk. The force of his hand smacking down sent pens and other papers jumping on the desk. "Goddammit, stop acting like a child! Give me my papers or I'll come around this desk and make you."

"*No.*"

If he could yell, so could she.

Vaslav's spine turned ramrod straight, and his gaze burned. "*What did you just say to me?*"

She didn't refuse him because she planned to keep his papers; he was perfectly capable of taking them from her, too, if he meant to. *Or wanted to.* Yet, neither of them moved.

And for a moment, she couldn't look at him. It

took more courage than she even knew she had, but Vera dragged her eyes away from his. Staring at him was easier … there was something magical about the way she found peace looking into his face. It terrified her, but that didn't make the phenomenon any less true. Maybe that was why it had been so easy for her to trust every word he said as long as he looked at her while he did it.

She couldn't *fake* content. That, at least, was real; the way it felt when she studied the plains of a stranger's face who didn't seem unfamiliar at all. Like she'd known him for her whole life. Even if she had not.

Home.

"At f-first," she struggled to say through the sudden chatter of her teeth, and her only show of nerves, "I didn't even know what I was looking at. Maybe that's why I kept flipping the brain imagery scans over. Just trying to figure out why there was so many and—"

"That is enough."

His every word *snapped*. Like the crunch of his teeth between each word was a slap landing against her face. Maybe the real slap would have felt better.

Why did he keep lying?

Why did he feel like he had to with her?

Vera *wouldn't* be quiet. As she flipped the pages back to the one that started her spiral of horrified understanding, she lifted it for him to see, thrusting it forward. Even though she couldn't see the words printed on the beige, thin paper, she couldn't forget them, either. When he refused to look at the paper, she turned it over and read it out loud anyway.

"*Mr. Pashkov,*" Vera read, "A simplified version of

my unofficial assumed diagnosis and prognosis follows. As agreed, your records have been destroyed, and no one had seen or accessed your file except for me. Regards—"

"I know what the goddamn man wrote," Vaslav interrupted before she could even finish the cover letter from the doctor who had even included his office's address in the city. At the same hospital where Vera had spent a handful of days not too long ago. Vaslav was even less kind when he spat, "He made me suffer through an entire conversation when he delivered the reports to me by hand. He's finally given up calling my fucking house every other damned day."

"When was that?" she asked.

His glare shot invisible knives her way. "Stop pretending like you had any business picking those papers up and looking through them in the first place."

"You left them out in the open, Vas."

"Behind a locked door, hence the mess. Mira hasn't been able to even get in my rooms for days. I left the suites upstairs unlocked for meals, but she knows better than to go beyond the gathering room. *You*, on the other hand, know *nothing*."

Vera's chin snapped up subtly, just enough for her to let him know she wouldn't cower at his insults or his mood. "Would you have told me?"

"I only just found out myself."

The cover letter from the doctor had been signed at least two months ago. Some of the dates on the reports, especially the imaging of Vaslav's brain in everything from grayscale to three-dimensional color, had gone back over a year. It wasn't that she didn't believe what he said to be true; when she considered the dates of the MRIs and other medical testing documents, however, Vera didn't think that Vaslav was telling her the whole story.

"What did you think it was?" she asked.

"How much did you read?" he shot back.

The retort wasn't as hot as his earlier ones. Maybe because she heard the pain that soaked it.

"Why can't you just answer the question? Just answer even *one* of my questions. *Please.*"

As hard as nails, he had the nerve to ask, "Why should I? You didn't have the decency to give me privacy; I don't *owe* you anything."

Bullshit.

"Get off it," Vera replied just as fast. "You want to talk about pretending? Then let's not pretend you're the kind of man who assumes he can trust people until they prove him differently. If the papers were out, you expected *somebody* to see them. Whether or not you meant it to be me is an entirely different story."

"*Me!*" he exploded. "I had them out for me!"

The loud shout startled her in the chair. It was nothing compared to the crash of the items on his desk, and the desk itself, made when he used both hands to lift the piece of large furniture over to its side, and then on its top. Frozen in her seat, only her chest moved when she took a few, shaky breaths. Vaslav, on the other hand, *paced.*

Like a caged animal.

Wild, and mean.

All at once, he stopped and pointed a single finger at her. He didn't even act like he'd ruined the desk and every item on or inside it, never mind that it laid just feet away. It was as if the furniture still sat between them. The only thing keeping him from crossing the space to get to her even though she found hatred there.

"You had no right," he uttered.

Betrayal clung to his heavy brows.

Vera hadn't expected the last piece of her puzzle to click together at that moment. When she found the papers, complete with a short, succinct cover letter and a typed, one-page explanation of a probable progressive, and aggressive, brain disease, she stupidly thought she had it all figured out. Or rather, that she had him figured out.

She didn't.

Until that very moment.

He didn't *want* her to know.

She bet that he didn't want anyone to know, really, but especially not her. When the list of symptoms included things like behavioral and personality changes; when it ranged from confusion, aggression, paranoia, and even violence—well, one saw Vaslav a little differently.

Vera sure did.

The man she knew could make another cower from just his presence alone. Every off-handed remark that had been made about everything from his nickname to his cold demeanor fit the mold of exactly what Vaslav Pashkov wanted everyone else to see.

Because they couldn't see *him*.

Not the human.

The man.

Him.

"Would you at least tell me what you thought it was?" she asked quietly.

Had he noticed the tears that tracked lines down her cheeks? She couldn't think of a reason to wipe them away.

Vaslav scoffed, and slapped his thigh overtop the towel that hadn't come loose in his earlier rage. *Somehow.* "Isn't it always cancer?"

"Your humor is offensive."

"I didn't say it was fucking funny."

Vera sucked in a sharp breath, and raised the papers a bit higher as she asked, "Would that have been better or worse to you than this?"

All the fight in Vaslav left the moment that question left her lips. He hadn't been expecting her to ask it if the lift of his brow was any indication, but the man was terribly good at hiding his emotions.

"It would have been final," he said. "I at least wanted that. To know for sure. I could go somewhere from there."

Right.

He probably felt like he couldn't go anywhere now.

Vera remembered what the doctor had included in his letter to Vaslav that was basically a simple report to explain what he believed the brain disease to be and why he thought it was so. Apparently, something like chronic traumatic encephalopathy wasn't confirmed until after death when the brain could be removed and studied.

It was only after the appearance of many symptoms ranging from mental to physical, all of which Vaslav had just based on what Vera understood to be true about him, and specialized testing to rule out other known diseases and illnesses, on top of a pattern of documented, repeated brain trauma, would a doctor make an assumed diagnosis of CTE. It still couldn't be verified until after death, though.

When she was a professional ballerina, Vera had been at least partially aware of the sports world for a time. Through competition, and the like, she was often kept informed on the topics that mattered amongst the elite athlete circle. The very acknowledgment of CTE as a real disease being found in the brains of famous football players, boxers, and even some veterans that had suffered multiple brain injuries during their service, was a huge debate that still wasn't entirely over.

Vera was not completely unaware about what she had found in Vaslav's office. It simply never occurred to her that she could somehow tie that disease to him.

Now, she couldn't unsee it when she stared at him. Vera couldn't sit there and act like she didn't know what she did. That his future would be bleak at the very least, and tragic at most. Early on-set dementia was a real possibility, but so was chronic, debilitating depression and even suicide.

The doctor had made it a point to note to Vaslav in his short report that medication and monitoring would be helpful for both those things. She bet he hadn't taken either of those suggestions well.

"How many brain injuries have you had?" she asked.

His left eye squinted in obvious irritation. "You think I've kept track between what, the metal ladles my mother cracked me in the head with when I was kid, or the cement walls that guards made my best and most acquainted friend?"

"Well, is there a definitive start and end to it?" She considered the confusing question, mostly brought on by the stark reality he laid at her feet about his previous abuse, and clarified, "A timeline of ones you can point back to? I mean, if you remember *those*—"

"*Don't do that*! I'm not here to go over history with *you*."

"Stop yelling," she said calmly.

It took more effort than she cared to admit. She willed herself to show him the compassion he so clearly struggled to find for everyone else around him. It wasn't his fault, though. Not one goddamn thing that made up the horrifying, terrifying spectacle that was The Beast of Moscow to the world was his fault.

The very thought sobered Vera.

She couldn't help but ask, "What happens if all the people who are scared of you find out you're not a homicidal maniac living out in the woods, you're just ... *sick*?"

"Shut your mouth."

He hissed every word.

Vera blinked down at the papers she still held, and more tears gathered on her lashes and fell. "I bet, nothing good," she continued like he hadn't said a thing. "I bet, you know it, too." He gestured with the papers again. "I bet knowing it doesn't help with the symptoms, does it? The paranoia and the erratic, destructive behaviors. That's why your doctor destroyed your files; why you wouldn't even tell the truth to me."

What could *she* do?

How could she hurt him to simply *know*?

Vera looked back up at Vaslav then only to find he blankly stared at the wall somewhere behind her head. His distant expression and lack of attention didn't stop her from saying, "Making everything about it disappear won't actually make it go away, Vas."

"I know," he whispered.

But treating it would also make him vulnerable. She didn't need to hear him say it. That didn't mean it made sense to her.

"You'd rather suffer and deteriorate alone than risk people knowing you're sick, even if it means you could have more good years?"

Better years.

Years he intended to spend with her, apparently.

Vaslav gnashed his teeth. The sound pained her, but she didn't show it. It was the sardonic sneer that stretched his cheeks, and put his scar on prominent display, that cut her deep. Especially when he said, "See, that's the thing, I won't be alone. Isn't that why I have you?"

If he meant it to sound cruel, the tone did the job. If only he could comprehend the way it sliced at her heart to know he thought she would only stay if he made her.

He didn't wait for her to respond.

Maybe he didn't care.

Vaslav fisted the towel around his waist to keep it in place as he stepped over the mess on the floor, and headed for the back hallway where he'd first come into the room. She heard his footsteps pad down that hallway to the stairwell at the back before they fainted as he climbed the stairs back to his rooms.

She was left in chaos.

Surrounded by his anger and destruction.

"And all because you wanted to help," she said to the empty room.

The room seemed to exhale the swell of tension and anxiety that had filled it full. It left her feeling even more alone.

A scary state, considering the alternative that waited for her upstairs. Even then, she wanted to be with him more than she needed to sit there holding papers that also wouldn't change a thing. Of course, she understood.

She had looked right through the beast's mask that was only there to hide the man, and the complex, guarded, *hurting* soul she found underneath was not at all what she expected; she didn't fault him for holding his secrets and fears close. Never mind, how his soul called to hers. Even then, as she clutched the papers tighter to her middle and her tears fell more, she had to stop herself from going to him.

Vera couldn't.

Hadn't she done enough?

Not while his anger spilled out upstairs in crashes and unintelligible shouts. Not when he couldn't stand the very sight of his own presence, and even the light fixtures hanging from the ceiling overhead rattled from something else being toppled over.

He didn't scare her.

His rage didn't keep her away. That's not why she waited. Everyone was entitled to their peace, and Vaslav was allowed his private pain. *Alone* if that's what he needed. Even if that meant sitting an entire floor lower than him, safe away from any line of fire, was what killed her the very most.

Didn't he know?

She'd hold him when he cried, too.

If only he'd let her.

7.

Thwack.
Smack.
Thwack.
Smack.

Vaslav became lost in the rhythmic noise of the mallet hammers whacking in unison as the sound echoed over the lake. The final two thuds of his hammer, and his companion's, coming down on their respective post stakes sounded different than the harder initial whacks.

Sturdier.

He moved for the pile of remaining stakes, only a half of a dozen, but the other man working side by side with him opted not to move. Passing the quiet Demyan a look as Vaslav chose his next post, he found him studying the peaceful water with fondness.

"My family has a lake property," he said without warning.

It was the first piece of conversation either man

offered the other that morning. Demyan's *fifth* staying on the property.

"That so?" Vaslav asked.

Demyan nodded absentmindedly, but otherwise, he didn't pay Vaslav any mind as he went about tapping in the first six inches of the sharpened end of the stake where he'd marked the next hole six feet away from the last.

"Kept in the family," Demyan explained. "The lake isn't as large as this one. It's fed by a similar landscape, the mountains."

That was news to Vaslav. In all the research Igor had managed to do on the Avdonin family, a private lake property wasn't one of the things to come up. Then again, if one looked on the deed of Vaslav's home and property, there wasn't any mention of a guesthouse, either. On purpose, of course. What people didn't know wouldn't hurt them.

"Ah," Vaslav grunted, letting his first swing of the mallet come down hard on the flat end of the post. His companion remained silent and pensive while Vaslav worked on getting the post in. After he finished, the stake took an extra couple of whacks to get past a difficult section of hard-packed ground, Demyan still hadn't moved to continue working. "Are we working, or talking?"

That caught the man's attention.

"It's not like you offer breaks," came the retort.

It wasn't even a hot one.

Vaslav barked a laugh. Those words coming from the same man who had already been shirtless and halfway through what remained of the posts before seven in the morning was a joke. "Let's not pretend like you don't like the work, comrade. You were the one up before the sun was to pound these in. I hadn't even got down here yet, hmm?"

"A fair point."

He thought so.

Still, the man didn't move. Demyan had little to no interest in continuing the work of pounding in the last few stakes around the lake. In only a handful of days the two of them managed to surround the lake in the bare bones of what would become the fence. The project had started two years earlier when Vaslav began cutting trees and stripping the logs of bark to let them weather. That should have taken a year, at most.

Instead, it ended up being another.

The migraines kept him inside more often than they allowed him out. A shame, really, considering how much physical work helped Vaslav to deal with everything. From his constant, overwhelming emotions to the almost compulsive urges that rarely led him down beneficial paths, just getting outside to *do* something helped it all.

"What's the problem?" he asked Demyan. Gesturing at the pile, Vaslav added, "We're about done. I didn't expect to get the perimeter of the lake done this fast. Either side of the road leading up to the house is next, yeah?"

Demyan squinted at him. "I'm not staying that long."

"Good."

That reply sent his companion's brow shooting up.

"You're not a bad guest, though," Vaslav added quickly.

Just so it was clear.

"I can't say the same," Demyan said, shrugging one

bare shoulder as he reached for the gray button down he'd left hanging from the handle of a spaded shovel he'd stuck into the ground earlier. "You're a terrible fucking host."

"If you want a different reaction, then try a new action."

Like not showing up without forewarning. Preferably, several months' worth of notice. Not that he offered those details out loud. Demyan was a smart enough man to figure out all on his own why they were in the situation facing the two.

Demyan considered that for long enough that Vaslav figured work wasn't going to continue anytime soon. He ended up using his last fence post as a resting spot for his arms while he stretched out the knots keeping his neck tight and tense.

"Why *my* daughter?"

"Did you love her mother?" Vaslav returned just as fast. "What was that like having a newborn in your arms as you stumbled into proper manhood while her mother's body rotted?"

Demyan's gaze snapped back to Vaslav's in an instant, and he wasn't shocked at all to find the fire staring back from Vera's father. "That's some nerve on you. How do you—"

"What, know that her biological mother is dead? That your wife is not her mother? Do you think she wouldn't tell me those things?"

Not that it mattered.

Vaslav *had* the intel. Of course, Vera offered a personal perspective on the details of her very early life, but that didn't factor into the question he posed to Demyan.

Through a clenching jaw, Demyan admitted, "To

be honest, I don't know anything she tells you. I barely even know what she thinks of you."

Should that bother Vaslav?

It didn't.

"And?" he asked.

"*And?*" Demyan parroted just as sharp.

"That's what I said, wasn't it?"

"You're unbelievable," the other man scoffed.

"Because I couldn't care less if Vera chooses not to discuss personal things about me with her father?" Vaslav questioned.

"*Da*, her father," Demyan spat.

Ah.

The defensiveness said it all.

"I get it," Vaslav said, nodding more to himself than Demyan. He pointed a finger at the other man, saying, "Take that to her."

"Take *what* to her?"

He wagged his still pointing finger up and down. "*That.* How you feel," he explained, not hiding the disdain coating the final word. "Those sorts of things are not useful to or wanted by me."

Demyan didn't appear any more or less confused than he had only moments ago. "You don't hear what I'm saying to you at all."

It wasn't even a question.

"Oh, no," Vaslav muttered, pushing off the post and heading for the pile again, "I understand perfectly well that you have things to work out with your daughter, and while those same things may in some way involve me," he said with a gesture toward his chest, "they don't *require* me. Not my attention, or even a conversation. See, that's the difference between how you feel and something I need to deal with."

"Do you hear the way you talk?"

"Yes, like you're a child."

Who needed *slow speech*.

"It's okay," Vaslav told Demyan, "it took Igor a while to get the difference worked out, too. And now that I've pointed it out, I can get back to work."

"You're un-fucking-believable."

Again with *that*.

Vaslav rolled his eyes so hard he thought he saw the back of his damn brain. "Get a new line, or get out of my face. I have things to do."

He didn't even hear Demyan come up beside him until the man's foot landed on the next fence post Vaslav intended on picking up. He glared at the man's expensive leather loafers. They certainly weren't the type of footwear meant for the work they were doing, but to each their own. It wasn't as if Vaslav gave the man the opportunity to properly pack for his trip.

"Move your foot," Vaslav demanded.

Even he heard the dark edge to his tone.

The *warning*.

Demyan didn't listen. "If you don't give a shit that my daughter doesn't care enough about the man she intends to marry to talk about him with her father, that's your prerogative, but—"

"I will cut it off, Demyan."

"I asked you a question, and the very least you could do is answer it."

"*With* the mallet," Vaslav uttered through clenched teeth.

And it would only be painful for one of them.

A beat passed between them before Demyan finally, *wisely*, pulled his foot back from the fence post.

He saw the defeat in the man's eyes while he did it. His chest deflated as Demyan took another step back and scrubbed a hand down his throat.

Vaslav stood straight instead of picking up the fence post. His stance on whether or not Vera opened up to her father about the two of them remained the same, indifferent if she did, pleased should she not. The question Demyan posed to him, however, wasn't quite the same.

"I need a wife," Vaslav said simply; the only information on the topic he would give, frankly. His health and life, never mind the state of those things, was not Demyan's business or concern. "And she will more than do."

Demyan blinked between furrowed brows. "And what if she wants a marriage that isn't based on someone else's *needs*?"

"Why else do people marry other than needing each other?"

In one way or another ...

"Because they want to?" Demyan returned.

"Who said anything about me not wanting to marry her?"

"You're impossible to have a conversation with. Do you realize that?"

Vaslav stared hard at the man, but admitted, "It's something I've been told."

More than once.

That wasn't what Demyan wanted to hear. A *fuck this* might have been muttered but Vaslav couldn't be sure. Frustrated, he shook his head and waved a hand in Vaslav's direction before spinning on his heels like he might head for the guesthouse.

"Hey, we're doing a job here!" Vas shouted at his

back.

The man stopped, his back tensing. It took Demyan more than a handful of seconds before he finally turned around to face Vaslav again.

"What?" Demyan snapped.

His unwanted guest looked as if he was two seconds away from crossing the space between the two of them and going around with Vaslav. On another day, *hell*, Vaslav might invite Demyan to attempt a fight. He towered over the over six-foot tall man by a good few inches, but they were of a similar age and build.

Demyan had a handful of years on Vas at fifty-three, but he bet the man wouldn't hesitate to throw the first fist, either. He respected that about Vera's father. Like the fact he respected Demyan's ability to work for hours doing hard labor without complaint, and that up until this moment, the two really hadn't needed to talk while doing it.

They should go back to that.

Soon.

"*Spasibo*," Vaslav thanked his companion.

"What on earth are you thanking me for?"

"The help with the fence, for one. Having an extra pair of hands around this week motivated me to get it done since you seemed so inclined to get up at the crack of dawn and work with me."

Demyan's tight lips caused each of his words to be clipped when he replied, "It wasn't exactly like you gave me anything else to do."

Vaslav pretended like he didn't hear that. "And for your daughter, thank you for her. She's kind when she shouldn't be; beautiful when she's sad; and I haven't found a part of her yet that I would change. While I believe a lot of what makes Vera who she is came from within herself, there's probably a lot of it that also came from you."

Clenching a fist at his side like he was trying to rid some of the tension there, Demyan glanced over the lake. "Why did you ask me that about her mother?"

"Gia, was it? Curiosity."

"You could *not* point out things you know about me," Demyan replied curtly.

"Now you know how it feels. Multiply that by about a thousand when someone does it to me. I react accordingly."

"A lack of self-control is a poor excuse for *drugging* me because I knew my daughter was involved with a man like you."

Vaslav didn't see the problem. "But now we both know how to behave, no?"

Hopefully, it was a lesson they both could learn from here on out. Neither of the two could afford a personal connection to the other without it interfering in their private businesses. While it might benefit Demyan to say he had a direct line to Vaslav Pashkov in the criminal world, it would only last as long as it took for Vas to pay the bounty.

"Yes, it was Gia," Demyan said then with a single nod before his gaze swung back to Vaslav. "I'd known her since I was a boy. Barely as tall as my father's knees. She's my first memory, and then she was my last for a long time, too. I've respected you enough to put up with your madness while I was here, I know good and damn well why they call you the beast, so give me enough decency not to poke a raw nerve just because you have access to it."

Vaslav flinched.

Demyan didn't catch it.

"Then, I'm sorry," Vaslav said.

"For what?"

"Asking at all."

Demyan cleared his throat, clearly uncomfortable at the turn their conversation had suddenly taken. "Is that your way of saying your question about Gia was cruel?"

"Or my way of saying I won't do it again."

It took a few seconds.

Eventually, Demyan nodded, muttering, "That's appreciated."

"Seems we have that in common, you and me. Love's tragedy."

It was the first time Vaslav hinted toward his first wife. He never even offered Irina's name, didn't plan to, and he tried not to consider if Demyan had found any information about his first marriage, and how it ended.

Not wanting to give the man time to prod on a topic that could very well cost him his life, Vaslav asked Demyan, "Anything else you want to say to me?"

"Is that an open invitation?" the man questioned. "Because yeah, I got a few things."

Vaslav actually considered the request, and settled on, "Within reason."

"Sounds like a death wish."

"Pick your poison," Vaslav offered with an open-armed shrug.

Demyan's stance loosened as he chuckled. "You know what, all right, I'll tell you what's on my mind."

"Is that going to get us back to the posts?"

The man acted like he didn't even hear Vaslav.

"I'm not impressed that my almost twenty-seven-year-old daughter has gotten involved with a man nearly twice her age for reasons that aren't entirely clear to me, has apparently taken little time to get to know said man, and has since decided to marry that man. And before you tell me to take that back to her, I'm not looking for your opinion on it, it's just an observation that I would like you to be aware I have made. If you expect me to trust that she's making her own choices and happily so, then that's going to be difficult considering the way you behaved with me. All things considered, because it's a lot, just to be fair."

"Reasonable," Vaslav said.

"And before I forget," the man added.

Vaslav smirked. "What's that?"

"If I don't have a return date for my wife relatively soon, you're going to have a second guest show up on your doorstep with even less warning than I." Demyan twirled a finger between them, laughing dryly before he said, "And let me say, she's not meant for this kind of shit."

It was only the song of the woods that whispered between the two men or a beat or two.

"I'll have a flight chartered within a day or two," Vaslav said, "and I'll make sure the wedding trip is not as … distasteful. That feels like a good word for it, no?"

Demyan barked out a laugh, shocking Vaslav at the suddenness. "Less illegal, but who really gives a damn about that?"

Even *he* laughed at that.

Vaslav gestured to the remaining posts. "Are we working?"

"I still want a break."

From him or the work?

Vaslav opted not to ask; he didn't care. "Fine. And about Vera …"

Demyan arched one brow higher than the other. "Yeah, I'll take all the rest back to her, huh?"

Right.

All those *feelings*.

That wasn't what Vaslav meant, though.

"She's safe with me," Vaslav said.

And where she needs to be.

Demyan's cheek twitched, and his jaw worked like he was chewing on the words to keep them from spilling from his mouth. It didn't last long, but what came out wasn't as bad as Vaslav thought it might be. Lucky for them both.

"Knowing what I do about you," Demyan returned, "forgive me for not trusting that to be true."

"Well," Vaslav replied just as swift, "nobody said you had to."

Hadn't he made that clear?

8.

An unexpected thunderstorm rolled in on the morning of Demyan's departure. The heavy, whipping winds and torrent of rainfall kept Vera hidden beneath the safety of the entrance alcove of the main house while Igor rushed through the sheet of falling water to pack the one piece of luggage her father brought along into the back of a waiting SUV.

She didn't see the point in rushing. The rain soaked him, anyway. It didn't matter to Igor. He wasn't even tasked with carrying the luggage but proclaimed all the same that it would give the father and daughter duo on the steps a chance to say goodbye in private.

Without the rain.

It was strange the way rain and wind could make the world look grey around her. All the color of the fall seemed to bleed away while the sky cried.

The majority of the thunder and cracks of lightning had already passed them by, and it didn't appear like what remained of the shitty weather would keep her father's flight grounded for an extended period, so he opted to leave on time, as planned. Beside her on the steps, dry under the small alcove, Demyan said nothing as Igor slammed the rear hatch of the SUV down and headed for the driver's seat.

"That's that," Demyan said, glancing her way. "Looks like my ride is ready."

"But not you," she replied. "You're not ready."

Vera could tell.

It was all in the eyes, her father's eyes, that was. Like hers, she found that Demyan's eyes were often the window to his soul when he was staring into the face of someone he loved. Open, deep, and *true*.

"Are you going to sell the villa?" her father asked, not acknowledging what she'd already said.

Vera shrugged. "I might."

"Or?"

"Real estate is a good investment, I hear."

Especially real estate in Moscow. Vera had no plans on getting rid of the villa after she married Vaslav if she wouldn't make double the price she had paid for the place, but that wasn't important at the moment. There were a million other things on Vera's mind besides her home in the city that had no leans against the property.

Demyan's brow creased. "I'm not sure if you're purposely avoiding my question, or—"

"No, I answered truthfully. I *might* sell it—or I might not. I don't know, and it's not on top of my list of priorities now. I have other things to worry about."

And handle, she thought.

Demyan nodded and turned to peer back over the front drive and the towering birch trees that leaned hard with the strength of the wind. It was only the deep set of the alcove leading into the front door, that Vaslav had recently repainted a fresh maroon, by the looks of the paint strokes on the framing, that keep them far enough away from the wind that it didn't carry their words away with it.

"Right," he eventually replied. "You're going to have a busy few weeks. Planning a wedding and whatnot, huh?"

His almost clipped tone made Vera pause.

"Amongst other things."

Demyan sighed. "I *will* be back for the wedding."

"Good. Someone needs to walk me down the aisle."

She couldn't imagine doing so without her father.

"I wish you weren't so indifferent—"

"*Who's* indifferent here?" she asked.

Demyan's gaze turned on her, then. "You sound like him—do you realize that?"

Vera blinked. "No."

"You do, and I'm not sure if it's a good thing or not. You talk like you know exactly what you want, and you don't give me any room to wiggle in an argument. It just is what it is, and you're not even stopping long enough to ask if I care."

Was that what he wanted?

Would it make him feel better?

"Do you not want me to get married?" she asked.

"I didn't say *that*."

"Do you not want me to get married to *him*?"

Demyan's lips pressed into a thin, grim line. "Vera, you're not being fair."

"How so?"

"For one, because instead of having an actual conversation, you just keep asking questions to keep this going in circles. I never said that I didn't want you to get married. You should do what you want to do the same way you always have. No, I don't expect you to consider my feelings or wants when you make decisions about your life because frankly, you never have. Some people might call it a selfish streak, but I never thought so."

"Why not? Isn't it?"

She'd never been good with that factoring in others to the paths she chose for herself. After all, they weren't the ones who had to walk it. That didn't mean it wouldn't affect them in some way. She was more than aware how that attitude could be taken as selfishness.

"Maybe because I love you," her father replied, "so any of those faults inside of you, I just … didn't see them that way. And there was a time, that first year after Gia died was hard, but as long as I was holding you, things were better. I don't think you realize that you saved my life a long time ago. For months and *months,* you were the only reason I didn't shove a gun down my throat and pull the trigger every single night after they took your mother from me."

A sharp breath burned in her lungs. In the week that her father spent at the Pashkov property, they mostly kept to safe conversations with only the occasional trip into dangerous waters. She had thought he didn't want to overstep his bounds, not with her, or Vas, but it wasn't like the week had been a good example for her father of what her life would be like.

Never mind, if she even wanted it.

"And so I decided back then, after things got better, and I didn't need to hold you at night just to keep from finding my gun, that no matter what, Vera, I was going to let you live. You weren't even supposed to. You should have died with your mother. The lack of oxygen during your birth should have killed you."

"I'm still here," she whispered.

"It's your life," Demyan murmured, "and I want you to do anything, *everything*, with it."

"As long as it's what I want," she said, hearing what he didn't say.

Demyan lifted one shoulder under his black blazer. "Maybe the issue is that I was never good at figuring out what it was you wanted, Vera. You were always way too busy running ahead of me to just grab it for yourself. That was my fault, too. I told you to do it."

"We've got five minutes to be on the road, comrade! Let's move!"

Vera hadn't even noticed that Igor rolled down the passenger side window to shout at the two on the steps, but it quickly brought her back to the bigger issue at hand.

"I know this seems fast to you, me and him," she tried to clarify.

Demyan let out a tired laugh. "Oh, Vera, that's not even *half* the problem."

"Okay, then *who* he is, or—"

"Again, not scratching the surface."

Vera blew a hard breath out, asking, "Then what is it? I can't read minds, and I don't want you to leave angry or sad. Not with me. It's not the greatest time, you know? I don't want to think for the next six or seven weeks that you don't want me to do this, because I *am* doing it, Papa."

"I know you are." Demyan smiled that same

comforting grin he used to give her when she was just a girl, and came shouting for him for one reason or another. When she needed her *dad*. "All of this makes me think I let you run so far ahead for so long that I'm never going to catch you again. Like you're not mine, anymore. You're not ever coming back to me, and now I have to give you away on top of it all, too."

She blinked again, but that time, a tear or two escaped and fell from her lashes. Her father was right there to wipe it away, already turning with a hand raised for his gentle fingertips to sweep off the wetness from her cheeks, and the following tears that fell, too.

He pulled her in for a tight hug. His arms suffocated her into the expanse of his chest and crushed her there until she couldn't breathe. Vera didn't pull away.

She didn't want to.

Until it felt like time stood still around them, and she couldn't even hear the wind howling or the rain pounding down on the ground, Vera didn't move from the safety and warmth of her father's hug. He kissed the top of her head, and rubbed a hand soothingly across her shoulders before he muttered thickly, "He's going to shout at me to hurry up again."

"Igor isn't so bad," she sniffled as Demyan pulled away.

"At least, he listens."

Vera didn't know what that meant.

She had other things to say, anyway.

"I love you, Papa," she told him.

Demyan's lips split with a wide smile. "I know, my *dushka*."

"And I'm not still running away. Not from you, or myself. Not from anyone."

"No?"

Vera shook her head. "I just found a place where I might want to call my home."

Or rather, a man that felt like the closest thing to it.

"I'm sorry if it's not the home you wanted for me, Papa," she added quieter.

"Vera, I only want you to be happy."

＊

Hours after Vera watched Igor drive her father down the long, winding drive, and a phone call with her mother that lasted longer than any in her recent memory, she was still sitting in the same spot where she'd sat to think after Demyan left. Staring out the sliding doors leading out of Vaslav's den, her questions for herself demanded more questions as the sunlight turned to darkness right before her eyes.

Mira had only checked in on her a couple of times, both for meals. She didn't refuse the food, but she wasn't in the mood for conversation. Thankfully, Mira didn't seem to be hurt by that.

Vera didn't even wonder where Vaslav spent his day after her father's departure because she didn't have to. Early in the late morning before, Mira had made her way down to the guesthouse to give Vera a message.

A particularly bad migraine hit Vaslav; he would see her when he did.

Along with the news of her father's flight the following day. She barely even had time to say goodbye before Demyan was gone on top of her worries swirling around Vaslav. Mostly because that was the first time he had gone out of his way to inform her about the state of his well-being.

Literally.

Every other time she was there, and he couldn't hide it. Because she fully suspected that his pain and troubles were ever constant in his days, *never ending.* Better or worse, well, that could be debated. She doubted he was ever totally free, though.

Like the past week.

How often was he bedridden?

Or worse?

And she was just down the hill …

It was only when the squeak of a shoe stopped near the den's doors did Vera glance away from the picture the evening painted in the backyard. She expected to find Mira had come to ask her if she needed anything for the evening, but Vaslav stood there. Hands tucked into a pair of black sweats, with a plain white t-shirt pasted to the planes of his broad chest, and dark circles under his pensive stare that zoned right in on her.

She frowned. "Are you feeling any better?"

"Not particularly."

As he spoke, his jaw worked around every word. Like it took a great deal of effort to form the words, and then, he had to get through speaking them, too.

Still, he asked, "Didn't Igor tell you that Kiril—"

"Would take me home, yes," she interjected. At the flinch in his brow, she lowered her voice another octave. Barely above a whisper. "I don't really have anything I need to be in the city for—no work, the villa is fine if Kiril can water the plants every few days, and … yeah."

"You'd like to stay here."

It wasn't even a question.

Vera nodded. "I would. With you."

That part needed to be clear. Especially as she watched Vaslav's gaze travel over the state of his den. The same place where they had first sat down for tea was unrecognizable from that initial meeting. What furniture had survived his latest bout of rage—when he toppled the desk as she sat in the office chair on the other side—was only a fragment of what she remembered being in the room that day. Gone was the glass coffee table with the ornately twisted legs made of metal between the couch and chairs facing the windows. Nothing remained on the walls. Every picture and piece of art depicting forest landscapes and snowy mountain caps had been taken down.

Or damaged, and then removed.

She didn't ask.

That wasn't the point.

Someone, probably Vaslav just from the sheer size alone, had reset the desk in its proper position on the large rug, however, they hadn't bothered with anything else. The glass bowl that had been full of individually wrapped taffy candy remained shattered on the floor with its sweet counterpart scattered amongst the rest of the wreckage from the desk.

Papers.

Files.

A pen holder, and all its contents.

The laptop and lamp.

Even a dried rose bulb sat atop the remnants of a night she wouldn't soon forget. Not because she had feared what happened, but because she suspected it wouldn't be the last time. It clearly wasn't the first.

Was it easier for him to just topple or ruin the closest thing he could get his hands on than to manage the way he felt?

"Are you sure staying here is what you'd like to do?" he asked quietly.

Vera rolled her teeth over her bottom lip before replying, "I'm not sure what you expect from me, but I won't be living apart from you after we're married. By *my* choice."

"But you might not always want to be here."

"So, I'll keep my villa. I *do* like the city."

He cleared his throat. "And you have the plants."

"They do need water," she admitted with a small smile. "But for the most part—"

"You want to be *here*."

He said it with a gesture at the chaos that had been left to sit for days. She wondered if that was because Mira didn't dare step into the room to fix it, or if Vaslav was just punishing himself by continuing to come back and stare at it all. What other reason would he have to let it sit and rot?

"Does that happen often?" she asked him.

Vaslav sighed as he scrubbed a hand down his mouth and unshaven jaw, but he nodded with a distant gaze locked and loaded on the mess. "It can."

"What does that mean?"

"Depends on the week."

"And what, the weather?" Vera asked sarcastically. She couldn't help it.

His explanation wasn't great.

Vaslav shrugged one shoulder, muttering, "Sometimes, yeah, the fucking weather, too."

Her regret hit like a ton of bricks. She didn't mean to sound like she blamed him for something he might not have a lot of say over.

"Is it just hard to control, or—"

"I don't always know I've done it, *kisska*."

She blinked at his honesty.

Words altogether failed.

Vaslav looked to her, then, and his cold eyes didn't seem as dark with the clear blue nailing in on her. "You might not always want to be here, Vera."

She hadn't needed him to repeat himself.

"I heard you perfectly fine the first time, Vas," she returned softly.

He scoffed. "Right."

"I did."

His jaw jumped against, chewing on nothing but his grinding teeth. Vera glanced down at her hands in her lap where she'd folded them. They gave her something else to focus on for a moment. At least long enough for the questions racing in her mind to quiet long enough for the ones that were loud enough to take center stage.

She didn't look up at him when she asked, "You're not dying, are you?"

"Not unless I do it myself. Which even that is easier said than done. Otherwise, I'm just slowly going mad and losing every part of me while I do it, *krasivyy*. Every day is something different. I put things in the same spot just so it's one less thing and ..." He dragged in a shaky breath, needing the extra air to say, "Someday I'm going to wake up, and I won't know anything about myself anymore. I'll have forgotten everything, and I won't even recognize the face staring back in the mirror."

But wasn't that just as heartbreaking?

She no longer found herself wondering why he

shut himself away from the rest of the world. How suffocating must his fear of someone knowing be if he wasn't even really *living*?

Vera glanced up from her hands when the sight of his shoes came to a stop in front of her on the angled chair. He'd walked over from the doorway without even making a sound.

"Even you," he said, then, so softly she strained to hear. The way he delivered that news without inflection made her heart squeeze painfully, but like everything else, she knew it was just Vaslav's way. It didn't matter if the truth hurt; he would still say it. "Someday, I'll forget you, too."

Maybe, she wanted to say back.

He didn't know for sure.

Couldn't possibly.

"I'll forget seeing you through the gallery glass. I'll forget the file that I have about you that I read every day just so I have it here," he said, pointing at his head. "And when you look at me like you do, when you think I don't see you doing it, when you look at me like you've been doing it your whole life, I won't even know that anymore, either."

But even so …

"I'll still be here," Vera said. "Even then, Vas. I promise. If that happens, I'll be here then, too."

She wished it didn't cut so deep when he barked out a laugh. "Yes, because I've had my hands in practically every aspect of your life these past months, I didn't exactly give you a choice."

Or she didn't need one.

Vera was entirely capable of choosing her own path. Why would he be any different?

She shook her head, not bothering to suppress the

tremble in her lower lip or the sniffle that escaped when she swiped away a stray tear racing down her cheek. "No, because I want to. I love you, Vaslav, whether it's your misery that loves my company, or it's meant to be … I'm here. And I am not leaving."

"Vera," he started.

Almost *placating*.

Vera tipped her chin up, her stare hardening. "Throw another desk. *Be mean*. Keep pushing. I don't mind pulling back."

"Stop."

She didn't.

"I'm not even asking for you to love me back, *ty zver'—you beast*, just that you'll let me at least love you." Vera gulped down a ragged breath that caught in her throat on the way down. "*Please* … please, let me love you."

That meant a lot of things. Vera didn't even think it would be easy. He wasn't an easy man, after all. She welcomed anything he brought with him, every single good and bad bit.

"Yeah, okay," he whispered.

Vera blinked, and another tear fell down. She wasn't sure she heard him correctly. "What?"

Vaslav nodded, and without warning, kneeled in front of where she sat on the chair. His head found her lap, and he turned his face to the side while his cheek nuzzled against the denim of her jeans. Her hands fluttered above his head, unsure of what he wanted or even what he was doing, before settling down one on his neck and another along his forehead. She didn't say a thing as one of his hands wrapped tight around her back, and the other clasped the top of her thigh.

"Okay," he said again.

Her shaking fingers stroked his hairline and the back of his neck featherlight.

"Okay," Vaslav repeated, as if he needed to say it again and again until he believed it, and settled into the softness of her touch. His upper body weight fell further into her lap. "Then, love me."

9.

Breathless giggles were Vaslav's favorite sound. As long as he got to hear it while Vera straddled him in nothing but her skin and a sly smile. Her skin pebbled from the cool air because he hadn't even given either of them time enough to wake up properly and get moving around before he'd pulled her black panties off to get better access to the heaven between her thighs.

The fire in the fireplace was probably out.

It felt cold enough for it.

He barely even noticed with her on top of him, and he didn't think the way she shivered up above him was from the cold. With his back resting against the headboard of the king size bed and his arms acting as a pillow behind his head, he had a good, comfortably reclined view of the woman attempting to tease him.

She was succeeding.

He wouldn't let her know it.

Vera's fingertips skimmed down along the swells of

her breasts as she rocked her hips forward and back again. The rhythm didn't stop. Every tortuous, slow grind of her wet slit up and down the length of his bare, hard erection tested Vaslav's self-control in the absolute worst way. He wasn't even inside her.

And that was the entire *point*.

"Are you fucking someone else?" she asked him.

He blinked and chuckled a bit at the frank way she'd asked him the question that time, but otherwise, he refused to move. He didn't touch her while she sat atop him and rocked against his body enough that every muscle was like a live wire.

Ready to snap.

The first time she asked him that had been a bit too rose-tinted for his liking. His reply had been something akin to, *just ask me if I am fucking someone else.* He got what he wanted.

"I'm not," he returned.

Sex took a great deal of energy. A lot of energy that he didn't care to spend at the moment. He barely even had to work for it with Vera. Just waking up beside her in bed before the sun had risen in the sky was enough to get his dick hard. Fuck the wind. He didn't need to hear that shit; her light breaths into his shoulder was more than enough to do the job.

Here we are, he thought.

"Then if you're not fucking someone else," Vera said sweetly with that same saccharine smile that made him want to kiss her mouth until she bruised and squealed, "I just want *you*."

"Go get the condoms."

She didn't move.

Actually, her hips rocked a little faster.

Her breath hitched, too.

Vaslav could have stopped her if he really wanted to, he preferred not to admit that fact to himself. Maybe he liked exactly what she was doing a little too much for his own good. And perhaps ... if only a *bit*, he wanted what she was asking from him, too.

"*Fuck*," he cussed low, a guttural moan catching in his throat when her lust-heavy blue eyes landed on his. "This isn't playing fair."

"Who wants fair, Vas? I told you—"

"*Yeah, yeah.*"

He knew what she wanted.

Didn't change much.

She sucked a hiss of air between her clenched teeth as he felt the warmth silkiness of her sex pulse with the increased speed of her tempo. She could get off like this—just rubbing her slit and clit, sopping wet, along his erection while he did nothing at all but stare at her. And he loved it. Every responsive sigh she made. Each time her long lashes fluttered closed because she found the right angle on the next stroke. He was as slick as she—just as breathless and desperate, too, even if he was better at subduing it— thanks to the way she'd been rubbing herself on him, chasing pleasure and teasing him all the while.

God.

Yeah, he knew she'd look even better with his dick disappearing inside of her, but this was what she got from him if she wasn't willing to play by his rules.

Hence, *the condoms.*

Her fingers glided over her public bone before dancing up his stomach. Every hard muscle in his abdomen clenched at the featherlight touch. He'd have given anything to feel her nails dig into his skin. Just a bite of pain would have distracted him from how good her pussy felt in those seconds. That was getting harder and harder to ignore.

Just what she wanted, too.

"Vera—"

"Can I come?" she asked, her voice pitched high.

His tongue tapped the roof of his mouth as an airless laugh burst from his lips. "Anytime you want, *kisska*. Get it out of your system, and then go get me a goddamn rubber to—"

"What is the problem? Do you want a panel of test results or—"

"I don't want *children*."

Instantly, Vera came to a stop on top of him. A shame, really, because not only had he been enjoying the bob and sway of her breasts, but the sudden ache deep in his balls signified he'd been a hell of a lot closer to an orgasm that he would ever willingly admit. He never did, but he didn't add that out loud. There was no need to rub salt in a woman's fresh wound unless she was a particular type of woman. Like his mother. Vaslav expected the news of his disinterest in being a father would land on Vera with the same impact it did on most other people.

He thought for sure she'd respond with sadness.

Instead, her blue eyes only narrowed, and a clipped tone soon followed. "Neither do I, which is exactly why I've had the shot for the last half of a decade almost, despite my doctor pointing out at my yearly check-up that I should change it to something more permanent. It's not meant for the *long* term, but it works for me. I don't mind the schedule, I don't get a period nine months out of the year, and guess what? *No babies.*"

Even just that word made him cringe. Baby.

"Don't make a face," she said, not missing his expression. "I didn't say it like I'm about to go out on a shopping spree for carriages and onesies."

"*What* are onesies?"

"Don't shout," Vera pouted.

"Then what is the entire point of this?" he exploded with a heavy laugh. "I'm pretty sure you just gave me blue balls all because we both want the same goddamn thing."

Vera tipped her head to the side. "So, why don't you get a vasectomy, or even better, why haven't you already? Don't tell me you're not capable."

The very best way to kill his mood in three seconds flat was talk of needles and knives near his testicles. He was not so prideful that he couldn't admit to being a simple man at the end of the day. Who would not be getting his ball sack cut open while he was awake to do it. And because he didn't trust any person in the world to have access to him while he was unconscious, surgery was out of the question unless it was literally life or death.

Vaslav shrugged and offered her a wink. "Because I'm not fond of cold hands."

Her brow puckered cutely before she glowered at him, and she slapped his stomach lightly with her palm when she realized he'd made a terrible joke. "*Stop it.* I was trying to have a serious conversation here."

Precisely.

And he was not.

"Vera, I woke you up to *fuck*," he told her, finally releasing his arms from their job as a pillow so he could grab hold of her waist. "The same way I've woken you up every morning that you've spent in my bed. The same way I would like to start *this* morning—especially because I have a very long day ahead."

She'd been so close to her orgasm just before she'd stopped. He'd felt it in the constant trembling in her thighs, and the way her focus lingered more on their connected bodies as her hips had started to pick up speed again. She'd been clenching her legs around him like a cage before she had to go and open her mouth. There was something addicting about the way she looked to him as she unabashedly chased her high, seeking her bliss in pleasure. The fact that she used him to do it made it all the more hot to him.

"And if only you'd shut up," Vaslav continued after getting her hips rocking on him again with the aid of his tight grip on her hips, "we can get back to what *I* wanted. We both know the truth," he told her, grinning like the cat lapping at the cream. A tremor worked its way through the bottom lip she was biting on while she stared down at him. "That's what you really want, too."

She sneered at him, then.

He laughed right back.

His sweet little kitten.

All fluff.

Tiny claws.

"*Prick*," she whispered.

"Yes, the very one you've been using to rub yourself off on, you *sweet* little thing."

Dirty, too. She was sinfully wicked working for her orgasm unashamed and wild. He liked her best that way. She talked less.

If only he didn't like it when she did that, too.

"At least tell me why," Vera whispered.

He swore he could hear the *please* on the tip of her tongue. The image of Vera begging while he flattered her to the bed, held her down on her stomach, and fucked her into another sweaty, humming mess filled his mind. Now, he just wanted to be doing *that*.

Instead, he settled on answering her truthfully. Hadn't she earned it? "Condoms give me control, you understand?"

Vera's fingers locked around his wrists, hips still bucking. "Doesn't change *anything*."

Vaslav opened his mouth to respond, but she was quick to quiet him when her hand landed on his chin. One finger pressed against his lips. He could hear how close she was to the precipice of her release by the high, hitched way she spoke and how tight and fast her rocking hips came along his cock while her warm, soft ass massaged his balls.

"It doesn't change facts," she said, the last word smacking from her lips. "It takes one sperm, that sperm doesn't even have to start inside my body, either. How long did you have me on my knees last night while you jerked off against my pussy? Rubbed me one out after, too, Vas—" His fingers clamped down harder, making her hiss his name a second time, but it wasn't enough to quiet her. "It *isn't* any different, you're playing with semantics because it makes you feel better. And I just want to—"

He bit down on her finger, and that worked. Not only to shut her up, but also to coax out the orgasm she'd been working on for minutes now.

Shocker.

His tender companion, all sweet even in her sin, sometimes needed a bit of pain, too. He didn't regret silencing anything else she wanted to throw at him when she was three seconds away from screaming her brains out, either. They could play a game of who knew biology better *after* she got off, frankly.

She kept one hand around his wrist, and the other slid down his chest as her hips came to a jerky stop while she cried out her relief. Pleasure hummed through every inch of her body as she wiggled on him from the sensitivity between her thighs.

"God," she breathed, still not quite ready to catch her breath yet, "you just had to do that to me."

"Well, you wouldn't shut up."

"I'm still not wrong," she shot back.

His balls ached again, but all it took was a single glance down to see the precum leaking from the head of his cock. The same seed he took such a careful effort to destroy ever since he understood the concept of passing his poison on, he didn't need a longer family line. Life was simpler when people didn't call Vaslav out on his bullshit, but Vera seemed to take every opportunity to do so as a challenge.

Most times, she probably wouldn't regret it. He couldn't make it a promise, though. This time, however, he wouldn't deny her what she wanted. His ego would take the hit and let her be right.

For once.

Pushing away from the headboard, Vaslav caught Vera with a kiss that left her weak in his hands. She seemed all too happy to be devoured with every swipe of his lips over hers. She was still shaking when his tongue speared past her open mouth to tangle with hers as he shoved her back to the bed. Her hair spread like a halo over the cream sheets, and she widened her legs for him the second he hovered over her.

Vaslav shook his head, saying only, "Oh, no, *kisska.* You wanted what you wanted, remember? I'm going to make sure I'm as deep in you as I can get for it, too."

He grabbed her hip to flip her onto her stomach, and only the sharp intake of her exhale echoed in the room when he hooked an arm around her knees, and dragged her ass higher. Not much, but he spread her legs wide again while he stroked his cock with fast, tight pumps of his fist. She was quite a sight like that, waiting and spread open. Slipping two fingers between her folds, he hummed his approval at the slick heat he found waiting for him while she squirmed as he toyed with her clit for a few hard circles just to wake her body back up again.

She would be paradise wrapped around him, bare, snug, and *soaked.* Vaslav couldn't wait.

And then she *wiggled* at him.

Or rather, her ass.

"*Hurry.*"

Her quip earned her the smack of his palm landing where her thigh melted into the swell of her ass. The bright pink handprint he left behind was as pretty as the hiss that cut through Vera's lips while her muscles went tight from her head on her toes.

"You hush," he replied.

"If you do that again, on the other side."

Vaslav laughed, and gave her exactly what she wanted. It left her ass with matching handprints on both sides, and he planned on adding a hell of a lot more while he palmed handfuls of her perky ass while he buried himself balls deep until he couldn't fucking breathe. He'd leave a bruise for every single finger on his hands, and he bet she would *still* ask for more.

Why couldn't he spend his entire day like this?

He wasn't asking for much.

The second the head of his cock was poised at the opening of Vera's wet slit, she was already trying to back on him, rolling her hips and ass into him to get even an inch more. Yet, he held her off. Even when she whined and her fingers curled into the bedsheets.

He waited.

Just long enough for her to relax.

And then he was *all in*.

One hard stroke, her body, already wet and greedy for more, took him straight to the hilt. He filled her with every inch of his cock until his balls were seated again damp, shivering skin. Her head tilted back, and a breathy laugh echoed from Vera when one of his hands cupped the front of her throat. His other hand pressed the small of her back down until her stomach was flat against the mattress.

With his feet planted on either side of her legs, he could get good and deep. Every pump of his hips came harder and harder until those whines of hers were a constant crescendo of moans that he wouldn't soon forget. Vera made beautiful music when he fucked her.

He couldn't hold her tight enough. Couldn't get enough of her skin against his. There just wasn't enough to go around—not of her smell, the way she looked under him, or how just being like this with her was more than enough to almost make him forget about the constant ache deep in the base of his skull. He swore the faster and deeper that he took Vera, every slap of his body against hers started to match the *thump-thump-thump* of pain in his head.

He could deal with it like this.

Didn't mind it as much.

"Oh, my *God*," he heard her mumble into the bedsheets.

Sweat slicked down her spine.

She clenched all around him.

Vaslav put a bit more weight behind the next flex of his hips; and he knew in that moment he'd been right. He could feel every single flutter of her inner walls and the way her muscles milked him the closer she came to her orgasm.

The thoughts of his pain were already a distant memory. Life had given him something far better to enjoy for the moment.

*

"Vas, did you hear me?"

"As hot as you can stand it," he called back.

The answer to her question on the temperature for the shower she promised to share with him must have satisfied Vera as the next thing he knew, the sound of rushing water spilled out from the attached master bath.

He should have followed her right in. Had she been a little more observant, Vera would have realized there wasn't actually that much of a mess on the bed for him to clean. A pile of sheets in the corner that Mira could wash and dry later. Nothing *terrible*.

The few minutes gave him time to think, however. Or rather, time to make a phone call. One he didn't particularly want Vera being privy to if he could help it. Not because he thought she would use it against him at a later date, either. He simply didn't want her to have to deal with his mother.

Not yet.

Early morning wasn't exactly the best time to call his mother, but he didn't care about her preferences when it came to him. Not to mention, he couldn't think of a single alcoholic that could manage to drag themselves, coherently, from a bed before seven.

Nonetheless, he stepped out of the bedroom and into the sitting room of the master suites as he dialed Natalia's familiar number. His mother wasn't the type to pick up on the first or second ring. He'd also added her contact to his block list in his cell phone so that by some chance she did manage to get ahold of his new personal cell number, he'd already been ahead of the issue.

That didn't mean he couldn't call *her*.

It would also come up private.

After the sixth ring, he started to think the call might go to voicemail, but then he remembered that the last time the bill came in, he'd ordered Mira to remove every extra thing from his mother's side of things. Including her voicemail, call waiting, and extra data just because he had been feeling extra spiteful that day.

So, he didn't hang up.

Vaslav let the phone keep ringing.

He'd come to stand at the windows overlooking the front property, giving him a good view of the entire yard, and the hill all the way down to the towering lilac trees and the gate at the very bottom. His mother picked up the phone after what felt like more minutes than he would consider acceptable for anyone else expecting a call from him.

Even if she hadn't been expecting it.

That didn't really matter.

"D-*da, da—chto ty khochesh'?*"

Vaslav chuckled, and silence fell over the line. "Is that anyway to pick up a call from your only son, Natalia?"

A phlegmy cough answered his question, and he swore he heard a piece of furniture squeak on the other end of the call. "*Vaslav?*"

"Who else?"

"It's—" Was she sober? He couldn't tell when her words weren't slurred. Then again, she could drink nearly a gallon of vodka in a day and still keep her eyes straight. "Christ, it's *barely* seven in the morning!"

"And?"

"And! *And?*" Natalia spluttered.

He didn't dignify that with a response. Vaslav wasn't a fan of wasting his time.

"I see the doubled monthly allowance has been a good enough consideration for you to keep your distance," Vaslav noted. "I appreciate that, *Mat.*"

Natalia sighed a shaky breath that cracked over the phone. "It's not like you give me a choice. You pay my rent, every other bill, *and* you're the one putting anything in my bank account lately. I don't mind being paid not to see your damn face, Vaslav."

Oh, he knew.

She proved that once when she used his money and influence to keep *him* locked up in a madhouse for as long as she could. The doctors that were supposed to help spent the majority of their time keeping him locked in a room with walls made of cement bricks and his typical daily outfit included nothing more than a straitjacket, and something akin to a ball gag that kept him from shouting, biting, or anything else useful. Her only mistake was thinking no one else cared about Vaslav back then. Too bad for her, it was also what got him *out*.

"I've been trying to get a hold of Mira for a month," she complained, then.

Vaslav massaged the spot between his eyes where extra tension had taken hold as he was forced to sit through her nasally voice. Even if it was just over the phone. Except that was the point … soon, the two of them would be face to face once more.

"I need a favor," Vaslav said.

He wouldn't engage her on the Mira issue. That was just one person Natalia could sink her claws into when Vaslav's back was turned. One of the only people close to him, daily, that could feed Natalia information she wouldn't otherwise have. Not that Mira meant to spill any of his secrets … she just wanted to please.

Too kindhearted, really.

"I'm sorry?" Natalia's tone changed all at once. Dripping with an oily sweetness that he knew was fake right from the start, she asked, "What exactly does that mean?"

Fuck.

She was already plotting.

He could tell.

The bitch didn't even know anything yet, not his favor he planned to ask, the recent changes in his life, or even the fact there was a woman waiting for him just a room or so away … naked, wet under hot water, and entirely *his*. All things he'd like to keep from Natalia, but Vaslav knew … it was just a matter of time before that ended.

What would happen then?

"Yes," Vaslav said, clearing his throat. "I said a

favor. I need one."

"Do tell."

"A dinner."

"What, with who?"

"Your brother," he uttered low.

Natalia took a second to respond. "*Who?*"

She heard him.

Vaslav refused to repeat it.

The chirpy, almost tickled, laughter that escaped his mother made him cringe for more reasons than one. She used to do that same laugh when he'd cry as a little boy because she was being particularly mean or rough with him, even going as far as enjoying the way he'd scream out when she bent his arms back at awkward angles simply because he wouldn't sit still when she demanded it. Every part of Natalia Pashkova was a trigger for Vaslav.

In the *worst* way.

His life would be a million times better the day he put her into the ground, but that would all come in due time.

"Oh, God," Natalia eventually said, sounding all too cheery when she asked, "What did you do now that you need to sit down at dinner with the Prosecutor General of Russia?"

"Right, my *uncle*," he reminded her.

The man would go to great lengths to keep Vaslav from spreading that little known information to the rest of the public.

"A bastard. Papasha *never* acknowledged him and—"

"*Mat*, I know the fucking story. I *promise* I don't give a shit to hear it again, either. Do me a favor and make a call. What do you want? Enough money to drown in it?" Or she could drown her *liver*; he wasn't picky on what she bought with any money he gave her. Vodka included.

Vaslav didn't particularly care to mingle in public with anyone, let alone a relative who had already previously agreed to keep his distance as long as he did the same. However, Vaslav was in need of someone within the higher ranks of the officials to pull the speculation away from him for recent bodies showing up in the canal. Less talk in the city meant less talk in the country; he didn't need his brigadiers getting too close to his business that they could see if something was wrong. Especially because *everything* was wrong.

With him, anyway.

The bodies were a problem he had not forgotten about. He'd simply put it off for as long as he possibly could.

"So, I'm waiting, we'll get back to the money," Natalia said, suddenly wide awake and willing to chat like they did it every single day. Nobody could call her a terrible actress. "What did you do?"

"Who said I did anything?" he asked.

"You don't have to say a thing," Natalia returned, cackling as if her entire day had just been made. "It's *you*, Vaslav. It's always *something* with you."

Bitch.

"Vas?" he heard Vera call from the bathroom. "Are you coming?"

He didn't know if his mother heard the woman in the background, and frankly, he didn't wait long enough to find out.

"Get me a dinner with the bastard, *Mat*," Vaslav demanded, his tone offering no room for discussion, and then he hung up the phone. He barely missed a beat with Vera, already turning back to head for the sound of the shower and her responding giggles when he called back to her, "Give me ten minutes inside of you, and I will be."

Again.

10.

"I thought you were grabbing your shoes from the den?"

Vera didn't startle at the sudden appearance of Vaslav behind her despite the fact she hadn't even heard his approach. Showing him the flats that dangled from her fingers, a pair Kiril had included in a bag he packed of her belongings, she said, "I did."

He seemed to notice the section of pictures in matte black frames that had caught her attention in the main hall. Vera never had the chance to properly browse the walls upon walls of images that spanned at least a century. There were more faces that she didn't recognize than ones she did. Until she came upon the ones of Irina.

Guessing by the similarly dressed people in the background, and the grand hall with sweeping silks hanging from the ceiling between large chandeliers, Vera believed it was an event of some sort.

She eyed Vaslav as he leaned a bit closer, needing

to come over her shoulder as he squinted at the small four by six inch framed images of his dead wife. Tall and thin, Irina wore a gown that accentuated her elegance with a bodice covered in multi-sized white pearls that contoured to her body from her hips up. Those pearls continued down the sleeves where they stopped at her wrists. The entire skirt of the dress, made of silk and sheer chiffon, billowed in wind Vera couldn't feel.

She smiled *brightly*.

Radiating from the frame.

The other images featured a handful of women that Vera didn't recognize and didn't intend to ask about. Only two of the pictures featured Vaslav scowling at the camera in a black tuxedo.

"I'm not fond of getting my picture taken," he said. "She wrangled me in for a few that day; it isn't every day you shake the hand of the Russian President."

"Are there anymore—"

"No, those are what survived."

Vera blinked. "Survived what?"

The way he was quick to move back from the wall of photos had Vera spinning around on her heels. Just in enough time to see the flinch race down the left side of Vaslav's face. He quickly rubbed it away with the pads of his fingertips, scowling all the while.

"You don't have to explain."

He dragged in a lungful of air, and muttered under his breath before saying, "We had a fight a couple of nights before she was killed, it's why I wasn't home. Part of the reason."

Foolishly, maybe, Vera thought he would say the other pictures from his wedding had been ruined in one of his fits. Had he lied and said exactly that, she would have easily believed him.

"She had them all displayed in the master suites, and they were fodder to fire that night," he explained, letting out the air he'd been holding as he spoke. Vera thought she might have seen a bit of tension release from his chest as it fell with the exhale, but he was terribly hard to read sometimes.

"Truth is," Vaslav said, staring past Vera at the photos that had been hung without any real rhyme or reason much like the rest on the main entry, "it wasn't even the third time we'd taken to throwing picture frames at one another and screaming across the room back and forth. Mira was just quicker about saving what could be salvaged after a brawl between the two of us by then. She knew how to manage that hurricane coming through."

Vera bet it was with a discreet quickness, too. After all, there was no way the woman who shared rooms just above Vaslav's private suite in the home didn't hear the things that went on between him and Vera, hell, she'd walked in on it more than once. Yet, it was as if the woman had an ingrained—or *well* learned— sense of minding her own damn business.

"The rest of these," he added, gesturing to the many, *many* walls of photos and family portraits, "ended up getting moved to the hall over the years. Some of it came from storage, and the rest came from different rooms I had renovated. Mira calls it my hall of ghosts. I find some of the pictures help me retain different things … memories, in a way. Or at least, the story of them."

Calling it his hall of ghosts didn't make it more appealing. Vera had other things to focus on, however.

"You told me you loved her."

A choppy chuckle muffled into Vaslav's hand. "I did, *too much*."

"But you fought—"

"Like cats and fucking dogs," he muttered with a dark laugh. "All the time, no? We had a way of picking at one another. Finding that pressure point and digging right in just because we could. I wasn't any better than her, it was like foreplay. She didn't know anything different, and I liked that meanness in her more than I should have."

Vera couldn't imagine craving a love full of volatility and viciousness. Never mind *needing* it. "Because it reminded you of yours?"

Vaslav nodded once. "In every way."

"How can you smile about that?"

"Am I? *Well*."

He even scrubbed a palm down his mouth but the grin stretching his lips remained. The thing was, he hadn't stopped looking at the section of photos, even as he spoke with her. Vera moved beside him and curled her arm in along his. Laying her cheek against his lower bicep, she said, "She looks happy there."

"I remember it being a good night. That was the first time we met properly but I had been in her circles for a while. It was all good, really."

"Even the bad bits, the fights and all of that?"

She glanced up to see his brow fall a bit at the question.

"Hurt people hurt people," Vaslav finally settled on saying.

"That's not a clear answer."

Vaslav shrugged, and leaned down to press a featherlight, and unexpected, kiss on the top of her head that made Vera smile. "Complicated things usually aren't … hmm?"

Fair enough.

"You should get your bag ready," he told her after pulling away. "Igor called. Kiril is ten minutes away, and he's in the mood to make the drive to the city tonight."

She had been shocked when he let Kiril take the ROV out for a rip just because the kid asked. Vaslav agreed on two conditions. Kiril wore the helmet, no excuses. He also had to stay off the neighbor's nearby properties.

"I could stay another night," she offered.

What was one more on top of the week she'd already spent alone with him? Not that every night was as good as the last, some were harder than others with his shifting moods and varying pain levels, but she didn't have anything to complain about. And frankly, she didn't have anything else to do.

Vaslav arched an eyebrow. "I hear you have a friend to see, and I *know* you have a dress to buy."

Vera's nose scrunched up. "You were listening to my call last night?"

She hadn't expected the late-night call from Hannah in Italy, but it made a lot more sense when her friend explained she'd finally gotten details about her ex-husband's funeral. Hannah intended on attending no matter how much Vera tried to convince her friend that it might not be a good idea.

Hannah wasn't hearing it.

I need this, she'd told Vera. *I need to know it's real.*

How could she argue with that? In the end, Vera offered Hannah a place to stay so she didn't have to room in a hotel for a couple of days, and even to attend the funeral of Viktor Antonovich. As long as her friend promised the two could stay out of sight and out of the way while they did it.

"Hannah sounded *very* upset," Vaslav noted.

He had the nerve to look serious.

Not at *all* guilty of eavesdropping.

"Knock it off, Vas."

He smirked, saying, "Listen, you have things to handle, and you might as well take the time to do it because you can't get anything done here with me."

He wasn't wrong.

Vera had an event coordinator to find to plan a small wedding in a very short amount of time. Vaslav had already made it clear where he wanted the wedding to take place, and the man he intended to marry the two of them. If those things were already settled, and Vera didn't really have a reason to argue about it, then that made some things simpler for her. She still needed to return to The Swan House to get what remained of her things. The longer she left her belongings in the locker, the better chance she had of not getting it back. Even if it was just an old pair of ballet shoes she couldn't even wear and a change of clothes ... that didn't matter to her.

It was still *hers*.

Feliks might have proven how much Vera was worth to him, but she wouldn't give the bastard anything extra in the meantime.

"I'll still be here when you get things rounded up," Vaslav said. "Hell, I might even drop in for a date."

That had Vera brightening. "A date, like ..." She waved a finger between the two of them. "With me and you?"

"Da, yes."

Vera shut one eye. "*Really?*"

He didn't seem like the type considering the amount of effort he put into *staying* at home. Literally. While the people around him, Igor, Mira, and even Kiril, came and went from the house and property without much fanfare, Vaslav couldn't say the same. She didn't want to call him a hermit, but he certainly wasn't living a very public life, either.

"If things go right," he settled on saying.

She didn't have a clue what he meant.

Then, Vaslav nodded her way. "Get an appropriate dress for that, too, yeah? While you're already out shopping for something white."

"What, a date?"

"Yes, a second dress for a date."

He was still on that?

Vera shook her head. "I don't know what kind of imaginary date you're planning so how—"

"It's not imaginary, *kisska.*"

"I'm just saying."

He gave her a pensive look.

She winked right back.

"At least tell me what kind of dress to look for," she said.

"Tasteful. Black. Formal, but not too …" Vaslav pulled a long face. "Black-tie."

"Like an event?"

"Oh, I'm not going to any event."

"But I need a formal black dress," she pressed.

He shrugged. "They're good to have."

"I already have five."

"Pick a new one."

"Are you paying?"

That earned her a sharp laugh, and almost like it

was on cue, Vaslav pulled an item from the back pocket of his slacks. "Actually, *kisska*, I am. And for anything else you might need, too."

He held the card up for her to see. Black all around with gold lettering that spelled out her name, the card number, and the expiration date, he spun it between two fingers, and then yanked it out of her reach when she tried to grab it.

"Does that say Vera *Pashkov*?" she asked.

He still held it out of reach. "Patience is a virtue."

"If you wanted a virtuous woman, you wouldn't like bending me over as much as you do." The amused shock that danced over Vaslav's otherwise stony expression had Vera grinning herself. She took his momentary distraction as a chance to snatch the shiny black credit card out of his hand before he had a chance to stop her.

Sure enough, Vera found it *was* her first name on the card. The surname, however, came from the man across from her. Interestingly enough, despite the two-tone double circles made of solid colors to say it *was* a credit card, there was no other branding to tie the card to a bank.

Vera opened her mouth to ask how exactly he managed to get the card, less interested now in the new surname, but he stopped her from saying a thing when his hand snagged her wrist in a cuff-like grip. He took one yank of her arm for Vera to stumble into Vaslav, and she swore her heart felt each of those shaky steps. The organ raced out of control inside her ribcage when the man flattered her chest against his when he pushed his hand against the small of her back, and he stared down at her.

"What?" Vera asked.

He didn't even blink. "I'm not sure what I want to do now."

"*What?*"

Just like a parrot.

Vaslav didn't seem to mind.

"A part of me would like to show you what happens to people who take things from my hands just to make sure you won't do it again," he said, his piercing stare skipping down to where her lips still curved with her sly smile. It was the way he sneered back, as annoyed as he was bemused by her antics but with a much shorter fuse than most people, that kept Vera in place. "And then you stand there, and you *smile* at me like you've won something, and that's all I fucking see."

Her brow puckered with her next question. "Is that supposed to be a bad thing?"

She didn't think so.

Vaslav let go of her wrist, he'd not taken the card back from her, but his other hand at the small of her back didn't leave, keeping her crushed against him. She felt every breath; for a man who didn't like to be around other people, he didn't seem to mind keeping her close.

She didn't get to look at the card again. He distracted her with the sweep of his fingers along the wispy pieces of her hair that framed her face. Then, he tapped the high point on her cheekbone with the pad of his index finger, making sure he gaze didn't move from his for even a split second.

"The card came in with the courier the day before your father left," he explained, that hand of his at her back tapping all five fingers like her spine was his personal drum to make a beat. "It was in the works the day after you gave the go ahead on a wedding. I'm aware you have a good deal of money to your name, and I won't even consider touching it. The card, however, covers everything else from here on out. There is not a limit, or a bottom."

"So no spankings if I spend more than I should?" Vera asked with wide eyes just to seem all the more innocent. As fake as it was.

Vaslav knew it, too. "*Right.* Just ask for that, yeah? As for the name on the card, you little *witch*—"

Vera's grin widened even further. "Tell me you don't like it."

Vaslav didn't miss a beat. "I didn't think you would mind if I assumed you'd want a more *western* influence on your marriage name."

She couldn't deny that he melted her heart into a beatless puddle with the news. It wasn't something she considered. This *had* been fast, and while a piece of her felt like it had known him her entire life … There was still a lot to learn. His consideration of her homeland was terribly sweet because he had proven on more than one occasion that he didn't think of others very often, if at all.

She knew better than to point it out.

Vera went the opposite direction when she asked, oozing saccharine, "Just what do you do to people that take things from your hands?"

Honestly curiosity made her ask. Her secret love of risks had her asking the question the way she did, however.

Maybe that was her first mistake.

"I cut theirs off," he deadpanned.

No, the question wasn't a mistake at all. Falling in love with him was.

Too bad she didn't regret it.

Vera lifted up on her tiptoes and pressed a quick kiss to Vaslav's still lips. Before he could even kiss her back, she was already rocking back on her heels. Waving the card that he didn't even look at, she said, "Thank you for this."

"I expect regular statements showing you spent money. *Reasonable* money, a coffee here and there just won't do."

Well, then. It was his money. She could surely spend it.

"Will do, Vas."

"*Come here.*"

Vaslav grabbed her wrist once more, but this time, it wasn't quite as tight as he tugged her up for another kiss that *he* demanded. She parted her lips only slightly for him to take what he wanted from her pout. The lingering hint of mint she found on the tip of his tongue had her senses buzzing, and his facial hair, filling in nicely again, tickled her with every stroke of his mouth over hers.

All too soon, he pulled away.

Vera wouldn't have that.

"Hannah isn't flying in for two more days, and the funeral isn't until Friday, anyway," Vera told Vaslav when he still didn't let her step back from him because his hand had not yet left her body. "I don't really care if Kiril doesn't mind making the drive tonight. *I* want to stay."

For as long as she could. And she didn't plan on staying away for much longer, either.

Vaslav's tongue peeked out to wet his lower lip as he murmured, "Then, I guess you're staying, *kisska*."

11.

"Did you know Kiril sleeps in the sitting room at night?"

Vaslav's daydream ended the second Vera made her presence known. While moving light didn't typically help his migraines, there was something about the flickering of a fire in a dark room that helped to pull him further into his mind and away from the physical presence of everything else around him. Including what hurt.

"Igor mentioned it," Vaslav said as Vera padded into the room and came to sit beside him on the plush couch where he'd found *some* relief. The fire helped. She set the plate of snacks, a mix of cheese, cut meats, and crackers, on the coffee table and produced what waited for him in her other hand. He eyed the small glass jar resting in the middle of her palm. "What's that, now?"

"Coconut oil."

Vaslav squinted at the white muck in the clear jar.

"Where did you find that?"

"Mira told me there was some in the pantry when I asked."

"Vera, I told you to walk around and have a think if you needed to, not to raid my cupboards and wake up the maid at one in the morning."

He couldn't help that she wanted to be awake with him at all hours of the damn night. Not that Vaslav would pretend that he didn't like it, that was a given.

"First of all," Vera started. "I wasn't even finished talking about Kiril sleeping on a couch in the sitting room when you have at least ten bedrooms available in the upper floors."

Fine.

"Then, let's go back to that," Vaslav said in a sigh. His focus turned from the jar of goo to Vera as he squinted through the pain stabbing at the back of his head and radiating to the front of his skull with every throb. "Kiril doesn't have the patience to sit still for the length of time it takes to drive from the city to Dubna several times a day, often a few times a week, the way Igor does. It's part of his daily routine with me. Kiril, on the other hand, only really needs to keep an eye on *you*."

She blinked. "That's it, just me?"

"He's certainly not here for *me*," Vaslav returned dryly.

That's what Igor was for.

"You know," Vera mused, "I remember my father being a lot more hands on when it came to his ..."

Vaslav narrowed in on Vera. "His, *what?*"

"Business," she opted to say.

He didn't think she'd call the *mafiya* out by name. She'd not yet.

Wisely.

"I doubt your father spent several years dismantling another man's organization only to earn himself a legion of angry, distrustful men who owe him money on a monthly basis like I did. On top of health issues that would otherwise ruin him if not kept carefully hidden," Vaslav said through a scowl. "I'm not living out the rest of my life like a sitting duck. I didn't spend the last half of a decade scaring the hell out of every man in my vicinity just to hide behind these walls cowering in my own fear. There's a reason that nearly every person who knows my name is all too happy to let me live alone in my house in the hills, *kisska.* And I don't mind it a bit. Trust that."

"Is that where Igor comes in?"

Vas stretched his neck back and forth to ease some of the knots he felt tightening his muscles, but it didn't help much. "He is my gun, my face, or my mouthpiece. Depending on the day. Someday, he might even be me, and I'm not against that particular idea, either. He's earned an easy life after dealing with me."

"*You,* how could he be you? What does that mean?"

Vaslav didn't intend on answering that question.

"So, basically, what Igor tells Kiril is what goes. And right now, he says Kiril goes where you go," he continued, "because that's where he serves everyone best. If that means I have to deal with him sleeping in the sitting room so I don't have to listen to Igor complain about the fact the kid whines when he won't stay in the apartment he has—"

"Where's his apartment?"

"Igor got him one in the same building where he

lives. Something else the two of them never shut up about." Vaslav remembered why he didn't like the politics of things like friendship when he was forced to sit through conversations between Igor and Kiril. Sure, it took patience to teach a young man how to be a responsible, respectable adult, but nobody said that was Vaslav's job. *He* didn't bring that boy here, but he was willing to use Kiril's blind loyalty to who he believed Vaslav was all the same. "What does that matter?"

Vera shrugged. "Just curious."

"What I should do and will, if they ever put the damn thing on the market is buy your old neighbor's villa, stash the little shit there, and I'll have one less problem."

Vera's brow dipped at the remark. "How so?"

"Then I won't have to hear Kiril run his mouth about how close Igor lives, and that he's nosy, and if all I need to do is give him a bedroom to sleep in when he has to be here, to keep you from talking nonsense, too, well ..." Vaslav waved a hand high to end his ramblings. "Problem fixed."

Vera gave him a tight smile. "Just say your head hurts and you don't want to talk."

A hard breath escaped him.

Still, he muttered, "Fine, my fucking head hurts. *Please* shut up."

That only made her glare.

"I said please first, *kisska.*"

It took *great* effort.

More than she knew.

Vera softened a little, but that might have been from the tense stare she found looking back when her gaze met his. His pain almost always looked like anger in his face, usually because he was mad about it; why the fuck did this have to be his life more often than it wasn't? Why did he wake up and go to sleep day after day feeling the exact same way? Death would be a better option, and that pissed him off, too. It shouldn't have to be one hell or another.

Except it wasn't like that with Vera. He still hadn't quite figured out how to stare at her and feel anger. Too many other things wrestling inside of him got in the war, too, and muddled him up in the worst way. She was that little slice of heaven amongst the rest of his agonizingly endless state of pained numbness.

Even when he didn't want her to talk.

"Well, you never promised to be a good conversationalist," Vera told him, but he was already digging the pads of his forefinger and thumb into his eye sockets to relieve the sudden pressure forming there.

"No, that I did not," he agreed in a croak.

There was no hiding the pain, then, or how swiftly it changed from one thing to another. The sharpness of the pressure was like a punch to the gut. With a wrecking ball. If a head could somehow explode from the inside out, then his was.

If it happened when he was on his feet or when he was asleep, it almost always chased him to the bathroom as his stomach revolted. Since he'd been feeling it coming on for a while, the lead up kept him from falling asleep in bed earlier because he knew what would follow if he did, Vaslav handled it better than he might have otherwise.

Another gusty breath rushed past his barely clenched teeth, and he still hadn't taken his fingers out of his eyes though he knew it wasn't a great option for pain relief. The pitter-patter of Vera's fingers racing along the shell of his ear and around to the back of his neck had Vaslav leaning into the soft touch. She was a blanket of warmth around him with his head in her lap. It took seconds of her light scratching and rubbing to get him to pull his hand away from his face.

"I'm glad you stayed another night," he murmured when he could breathe without feeling like he might puke. "That you stay at all."

"Me, too."

Her touch was like her voice when she whispered practically airless, barely there, but real all the same. It was just what he needed. Silent minutes ticked by, but he couldn't say how many. Vaslav had become so accustomed to losing time to his agony that he just expected it now. Something else for him to get frustrated over.

Vera didn't say a thing, continuing her soft exploration of his head and face with gentle, slow sweeps of her fingers. Vaslav broke the stillness first, muttering, "What was the oil for?"

Her quiet laugh rocked him a bit in her lap, and Vaslav opened his eyes, despite the blinding pain that accompanied the action, to find Vera smiling above him. She shrugged down as her fingers swept soft lines over his cheekbones.

It was easier to breathe when she did that.

"When you first started into your mood earlier—"

"Right, when the migraine started."

Vera gave him a look. "But you don't say that until everyone else figures it out."

"Isn't that the point?"

Her nose crinkled. "Stop deflecting … earlier you

mentioned your face was itching. That the scar tissue does that sometimes when the beard comes in, but Mira couldn't find you more of the oil you liked. Coconut oil will do the same thing. You work it into an oil between your fingers, rub it on, and that's that. Something to try until she finds the kind you like?"

He'd only been muttering to himself, and apparently, she even listened to him do *that*. What kind of soul fell into his lap when she walked through his front door?

"Does it smell?"

"Not a lot," she returned. "But it definitely doesn't smell entirely like what you might think, either."

At this point, what did he have to lose?

"Try it. I'm not going anywhere, am I?"

Her chuff wasn't at all quiet, but he watched her with one eye closed as she reached over to grab the jar sitting beside her plate of forgotten snacks. The constant pain in his head was easy to get lost in, but all it took was the warm, oily hands of Vera Avdonin to keep him from drowning entirely in the waves. Closing his eyes once more, Vaslav settled into her lap and touch. If she wanted to be there, who was he to tell her to go to bed?

"And I didn't wake Mira up," Vera told him quietly.

"I didn't really mean anything—"

"She was checking on Kiril."

"*Mmm*."

Shocker.

"I'm going to put some of this on your scar now, okay?" Vera asked.

There wasn't a single soul, except for maybe a doctor that he paid to do so, who would touch his face willingly. Not to mention, anyone who would survive doing it. Vera, on the other hand, asked permission like she already knew what his answer would be, but the consent still mattered to her all the same.

"If you want to," he returned.

"Wasn't that the point of me getting it in the first place?"

Vaslav didn't bother to respond to the obvious, and Vera went ahead with massaging the oil into the scar tissue that stretched from his mouth across his cheek. The gristly texture gave the scarring an almost-grotesque appearance when the beard didn't hide the worst of it, but the woman holding him had never been put off by the idea of touching his face. It was a big part of the reason he didn't care if she did.

Her thumb worked soothing circles over the scar tissue, back and forth, again and again. He wouldn't say he particularly cared for the natural smell of the coconut oil, but she wasn't wrong about it serving the same purpose as a specialty beard oil he liked.

"The itching is better," he told her.

He could tell by the way her fingers pulled through his trim beard that the oil had softened his facial hair quite a bit, too. His skin around his scar and the flesh inside his mouth didn't feel so raw. The migraines tended to make his nerve pain far worse.

"I think you'd like it with a bit of vitamin E mixed in the coconut oil," she replied, and he could hear the smile in her tone. "It would help the scar tissue a lot. I can make some?"

"Well—"

"If you promise to give Kiril a bedroom," she added quickly.

Vaslav popped one eye open to find a grinning Vera above him. "I already said I would."

"You didn't sound serious."

"I was."

"About buying the villa beside mine, too?" she asked.

Vas shrugged in her lap. "Yes."

"That's a little much, no?"

Ah, she didn't understand.

To be fair, Vaslav never explained properly, either.

"Vera," he murmured, settling his aching neck and head back into her lap and sweet touch, "let me paint you a picture."

"A picture?"

"In your mind."

"Hmm."

"Sound more interested," he muttered.

"I *am*!"

"Not that interested. With less volume."

Her tempting fingers scratched under his jaw, but he liked it all the same. "*Vas.*"

They really did need to work on her patience. He sighed, and even rolled his eyes behind his closed lids. "The villa isn't about you or even the fact he's agreed to his job to keep an eye on you. Those are things he's willingly chosen to do without any expectations beyond what he's already been given for doing so."

"Which is what?"

"Basic things that he needed, protection, money. If you want those kinds of details, take it to Igor. I only care about the kid's loyalty. And so, the villa would be, like the apartment in downtown I bought for him, is what I consider a gift. Of sorts."

"A gift," she echoed.

"I don't like to call them that. People get sentimental."

And then they had to make a production out of it. It was one thing to buy a person's loyalty. It was an entirely different thing to reward someone in a way that *provided* for them. Like a home for a kid who probably never had one of his own. Simply because he'd shown loyalty to a man who had done nothing to earn it.

"*Huh.*"

Vaslav peered through squinted eyes to see the way Vera stared off above him. Not down at him like he wanted, but away at something else in the sitting room that connected his master suites together.

"What?" he asked her.

Vera quickly glanced down, realizing her hands had stilled on his jaw, and pressed her thumbs into his back molars to help with the tightness and grinding of his teeth. It cracked his jaw, whatever she did, but it felt good all the same.

"I just wondered," she said, "if you do that because you actually give a crap about Kiril, or because—"

"Igor does," Vaslav said, "and at this point, he's my only friend left. I think that counts for something."

Or it should.

What did matter was that without Igor, nothing about Vaslav's life would be the same. While it wasn't exactly the life he had planned for himself, it *was* a quiet one. Which was more than he had asked for, really.

"Oh."

Whether or not she was satisfied with his reasoning for his plans regarding Kiril, Vera didn't say. She continued her massage of his face, jaw, and neck before moving back to his temples and scalp, and he was happy to let the conversation die. The time had to be crawling closer to two in the morning, but she didn't complain the longer he laid in her lap.

"Will Kiril always keep an eye on me?" she asked carefully.

His answer wouldn't be as easy to swallow. "Until I'm dead."

It did quiet her questions, though.

"What else is that coconut oil good for?" Vaslav asked, honestly curious.

Vera giggled the most heavenly sound. "Everything. Even lube."

Good to know.

12.

"You know, I was looking forward to a drive back to the city with Kiril," Vera said from the backseat.

It wasn't a lie. Despite his chatty nature, Kiril didn't mean any harm. She hadn't seen very much of him over the past couple of weeks as he came and went from the property without much interference from Vaslav or Igor since being given keys to a new car. Strangely, she missed him being around, putting in his occasional smartass comment, or lurking the property line, whistling for Marrow.

She hadn't seen much of the dog since her father left, either. Although, she understood the dog hadn't gone far because he howled a lot at night. Like the wind, his howls carried as far as they could go, but it never stopped her from falling asleep. Frankly, other than the dog, there wasn't much else to hear but for the rolling mountainous forests and maybe the wind and rain when a storm came barreling through.

She'd quickly learned not to worry about Marrow

… the dog was practically wild, and the closer he was to the house determined a lot about Vaslav's mood and pain level. She wouldn't lie and say she liked Marrow, but she enjoyed watching him from afar. The dog was easier to appreciate that way, and less growly and quick to snap.

The neighbors couldn't even keep chickens, according to Mira, likely too scared to shoot the dog because of who he belonged to, if they could even see the black beast slinking through their properties to hunt at night.

"At least Kiril has decent conversational skills," she said to her current chauffeur. Vaslav and Igor could not say the same, and Vera dared them to try.

Igor, manning the SUV from the driver's seat, passed a fleeting look into the rearview mirror before his attention was back where it needed to be. On the road. "Take that to him. I'm sure he'll be around your place by the time I get you there. That was the plan, anyhow. If it makes you feel any better, I think Kiril is fond of you, too, yeah? He's still young enough that he thinks anyone over thirty is old, and you're just experienced enough to realize that when you constantly live life on the edge, you never learn to see beyond what's right in front of your face. It works."

Huh.

"I take back what I said, you're not such a bad talker, it just takes a bit to get it out of you," Vera said.

Igor chuckled. "Thank you. I think."

She had not forgotten about Kiril, though. By the time she woke up, late in the morning because Vaslav didn't fall asleep until well after three, Kiril was already gone, and the makeshift bed he'd made out of

blankets and pillows on a couch in the sitting room
had all but disappeared. If he was supposed to be
with her all the time, like Vaslav had implied, then
what was important enough to take him away?

"Did something come up, or—"

"You're awfully nosy today," Igor interjected,
making his reflection in the rearview mirror known
again so she was able to see the way he'd lifted his
brow high. "Any reason for that?"

"Curiosity. Maybe I'm bored."

"Didn't you hear? It killed the cat," he deadpanned.

Vera smirked to herself, and shook her head as she
turned back to the rural landscape passing by their
fast-moving SUV. Igor had no issue with returning
his focus to the long road ahead when his passenger
no longer wanted to talk. Or so he thought.

She just wanted to enjoy the view.

One of her favorite parts of Russia was when
autumn arrived. Even if it never lasted for very long.

Every bright yellow, burnt orange, and fire-red leaf
that changed and fell was a different piece of a
massive, beautiful canvas that made up the
countryside. Roads that had certainly seen better days
connected small rural communities. One couldn't
really appreciate the entirety of Russia as it slipped
into the fall if they never went further than the city
limits, but it was hard to look away from the miles
and miles of the season's colors in full, fall glory.

It certainly made the nearly two hour drive back to
the city a lot more bearable. Especially when she was
trying to distract herself from the real question she
wanted to ask Igor.

The longer the silence stretched on, only breaking
when Igor hit a pothole that provoked a curse, the

worse Vera felt. Like she was sitting on bees. Unable to keep the question in any longer, she blurted, "When did you know something was wrong with Vaslav?"

A dangerous question, she knew.

It had become painfully clear to Vera that Vaslav's worst, and one of his most prominent, symptoms of CTE was his ever growing paranoia. It was why he couldn't stand to have people even talk about him when he wasn't in the same room without obsessing over it at times. She'd tried not to count the hours she noticed that he spent peering through the heavy curtains on every window over the last week. There was a gun in every single room. Not that she had pointed out the discoveries to Vaslav, and it wasn't like guns made Vera nervous. Quite the opposite, her grandfather had been a gun trafficker; her father later took over the family business. They had a special love for weapons, and their prominence in her life had left her almost numb to the sight of a weapon.

Except when every gun she found was *carefully* hidden. As if they had been put in their respective spots because Vaslav needed to know where each and every one was, but no one else would. She couldn't imagine that with the amount of time Igor spent inside the house, or even Mira, that they'd never stumbled upon one of the many weapons he kept hidden.

She didn't know how to admit to Igor that she worried more about Vaslav's easy access to the guns than she did the fact they were there in the first place. That, coupled with his almost constant paranoia, could lead to a very bad situation.

"I only ask because—" She couldn't quite get the

words out when Igor remained tense and quiet in the driver's seat, their vehicle still cutting down the miles of rural road at a speed she rarely tried to think about. Not if she valued her life.

"I know why you ask," he eventually muttered.

"*Do you?*"

At least, she always put on a seat belt. The belt engaged to keep her tight against the seat when Igor pulled off the road without warning. She didn't know if he hadn't liked her tone, or he felt the conversation was better held when he wasn't driving, but the tires slid over gravel for longer than she was comfortable before the SUV finally came to a stop.

Igor's gaze slammed into hers in the rearview mirror as he put the vehicle into park. "Vera—"

"I get it ... okay? The entire point of you is that you make sure he knows when someone is talking or ... *asking* things," Vera rushed to say, her voice strained because she couldn't stop the sudden swell of emotions lodging in her throat. "But I worry about him when I'm not sitting across the room giving him something else to focus on except what's outside of his goddamn windows!"

Igor turned fast in his seat and scrubbed at his forehead. Eventually, he unbuckled his seat and turned to get a better view of where Vera sat in the row behind him in the middle.

"Do you know," he started to say, stopping to pull in two deep breaths before starting over entirely. "*Do you know*, Vera, what would happen to me today if I returned you home safe and sound, and didn't immediately call him to confirm what he already knows? And I will tell you how he already knows it, too, yeah?" he asked, grinning although it felt cold.

His mirth faded as fast as it appeared. "Because I guarantee he has kept meticulous track of every trip to and from your home that I have made over the past months. Do you know what would happen to me?"

Vera swallowed back the nerves flapping like the wings of a butterfly in her throat to say, "No, I don't."

"Consider yourself lucky, then. Because I certainly fucking *do.*"

"Igor—"

He gripped the headrest of the driver's seat, giving him better leverage for when he pointed a finger at her, quieting her from saying one more thing. "Here's another thing you don't know, but goddammit, somebody's got to fill you in, sweetheart. Vaslav draws an invisible line in front of every person unlucky enough to give a shit about him to a degree that they've found themselves attached to him in one way or another. That line? It's where he decides if you live or die. It's *your* betrayal, whatever you do, you don't even need to have done it yet. *He* knows what that line is, and you won't until you cross it. It's different for everybody, and it's apparent to me that he's given you a lot more grace than everyone else, but don't for one second think it makes you safe because you lie in bed next to him, Vera."

Right.

"Because you can't tame a beast," Vera whispered.

Igor dragged in another heavy breath and released it through flaring nostrils. "I knew something was wrong when he asked me the same questions he had already asked me before, about me and him. The first time we met; why he liked me. Those were things I *knew* he knew," the man said, falling back into the seat and slumping further down. "But every so often, he'd ask me the same questions again like he didn't know. I tracked down his doctor, then, the one he'd started seeing a while back. I paid the man to get back on the phone with Vas, but it's taken almost a year for them to have a face-to-face conversation."

"Does he know you had contact—"

"I had to take a risk," Igor muttered fast. "I had just enough information to go on to do it. It was worth it. I've got the seizures under control, and he's not self-medicating with whatever cocktail he likes for the day. He's back to barking orders into the phone and when you're around, he actually gets out of the house. I consider that winning"

He was taking another telling her that information, too.

Vera thought that counted for something. She grasped on to the proverbial olive branch because she had a feeling that even with counting the people sitting in that SUV on the side of a rural road, she could use one hand to name the number of people who had the access and ability to look after Vaslav.

"It'll only get worse," she said, wondering if Igor even realized the reality in front of them. "It doesn't matter how unstable he thinks he is now or how many walls and trees he puts around himself to shut out the world, what's happening inside his head won't get any better. Especially not living like he does."

"Yeah," Igor replied, his voice a croak, "I know."

"Does he?"

That was the real question.

"Making him do things is one of those lines I mentioned earlier," Igor said "And I have a pretty

155

good guess about where he draws mine just based on history. I enjoy my place and perhaps that's another thing you don't understand just yet. Don't worry, I'll fill you in."

His head fell to the right, giving Vera a good view of the emotionless expression Igor leveled on her as he said, "I have been the right-hand man to Vaslav for a long time. It's allowed me a great deal of power and privilege inside a world you will never get to see, you should be thankful for that, too, they'd eat you alive."

She didn't even blink at the subtle threat. Whether or not he meant for it to be threatening was another thing, but that didn't change the way it made her feel.

"If what Vaslav wants to do is hide and wither away in the hills of Dubna with you by his side beside him to pass his time, then that's exactly what I intend to let the man do. *Comfortably*. We all make sacrifices for the life we've chosen. His has led him to where he currently is, mine hasn't quite arrived at what I consider a satisfactory end just yet, but at least he's given me some insight on how it will be, and I can't fault him for that. Because someday when the threat of him coming out of hiding isn't enough to control the kind of people waiting for him on the other side, I'll be the only one standing in the middle of the war, Vera."

"But why?"

Why would he *want* to be the man standing there? Vera thought she already knew the answer.

"You care," she said, speaking it into truth.

"Yeah, *well*, so do you," Igor accused. "I guess we make quite a pair, no?"

*

Igor hadn't lied. Kiril waited, relaxed and bored in his staple leather jacket, on the front steps of her villa. As they parked behind the black, two-door coupe that Kiril now called his, he barely reacted to their arrival beyond a lazy wave.

"I trust that everything we've spoken about regarding Vaslav will remain between the two of us," Igor said, his sharp gaze jumping to her in the rearview mirror as Vera unbuckled the seatbelt.

"Why wouldn't it?"

Kiril, who had already pushed himself up to his feet and was brushing off the knees of his acid wash, distressed denim jeans, looked their way expectantly. Vera's attention jumped between the young man waiting to be let into the villa, even though he was perfectly capable of finding a way in, and the man with his hands still on the wheel.

"Some people forget he's just a kid, is all," Igor said, shrugging one broad shoulder. "Even if he doesn't entirely look or act like it most of the time. Adult problems are better left to those who can understand their complexities."

"Yeah, I'm not one of those people," Vera returned dryly.

"Good," she heard him say as she exited the vehicle.

Vera didn't bother with her two small bags in the back because Igor was already heading that way. Instead, she made a beeline for the walk leading up to the villa as she dug the keys from the pocket of her hoodie.

Kiril tucked something away into his back pocket

as Vera tossed him the ring of keys. "Look at that, today you get to use the *legal* way."

The kid had the nerve to grin. "Didn't really need it, though. I already popped in next door for a drink of water and a piss."

Vera side-eyed the kid as he flipped through the keys. "Seriously?"

"The old man's plants needed to be watered, too. They don't know he's dead."

"Did you actually do that? *Water* the plants?"

"I will," he muttered, defensively. "When I go back later."

Vera chose not to push it. All the while, she secretly hoped none of their villa neighbors ever noticed Kiril's odd propensity for breaking and entering. It wasn't like he stole anything, but that didn't change what his behavior was at the end of the day. Dangerous and criminal.

Like someone else she knew ...

By the time Kiril found the correct key, he wouldn't let her help, and got the front door open, Igor had already produced the bags from the back of the SUV and deposited them on the bottom of the stoop. He pointed at them, looking only at Kiril.

"I assume you've got these, yes?"

"Of course," Kiril replied as Vera stepped beyond him to enter the villa. "And I've got something for you, too."

"*Da?*"

"Yeah. Found it taped to the door."

Despite not spending any time in her villa in weeks, and desperately wanting to reacquaint herself with the familiar floors and walls of her home, Vera spun right back around to watch Kiril pull a folded piece of paper from his back pocket and hand it over to Igor. The older man flicked the paper open and squinted one eye as he held it a bit closer to his face to read what was written on the paper.

A grunt passed his lips.

Half amused.

Mostly annoyed.

"Yeah, that's what I fucking thought, too," Kiril said like he could read Igor's mind.

"What did I miss?" Vera asked. "Was that on my door? What does it say?"

Igor lowered the paper and arched a brow her way. "You're still nosy, I see."

"This is where I live."

"It's not serious. Just a message."

That didn't explain shit to Vera.

"A message from who?"

Kiril swung his head in Igor's direction, already on pins and needles for the man's response. "Yes, Igor, from *who*?"

"*Shut up.*"

"You're not fun at all," Kiril replied, bored.

Igor eyed the paper again. "Feliks, Vera. He wrote to let Vas know that he would like his payment now. Whatever side of the arrangement he made with Vaslav is fulfilled. He expects Vaslav to do the same on his side of things. I have to say, if nothing else, Feliks deserves credit for his tenacity. He always knows what buttons to push with Vaslav. Never fails."

"Vas doesn't even know he left anything at all for him."

"But he will," Kiril put in, grinning, "and that the prick left it with *you*."

Igor crumpled the note into his pocket. Despite the fact it had been left on her door, Vera didn't see what was written on it, and needed to trust that Igor told her the truth. She didn't think he had a reason to lie.

"Which just means he wanted the message to get through faster," Igor said. "Nothing more, likely."

It didn't help the way Vera suddenly felt. Or the way Vaslav might perceive the message. Those butterflies came back with a vengeance in her throat, and deep in her belly, too. She couldn't shake the nerves or the anxiety that came with it.

"He won't overreact, will he?" she asked. "Because this isn't exactly a good week for it."

"Oh, right," Kiril said. "The chick, Hannah, she's coming! When is your friend getting in from Italy? I liked her."

Hannah was only one reason why it wouldn't be a good week for Vaslav to throw a fit. Vera didn't see the point in explaining all the other reasons why, too.

"You didn't even meet her," she said.

Kiril shrugged. "I liked what I *saw*."

"That's enough, Kiril," Igor muttered heavily. "Date girls your own age."

"Have you met girls my age?" the younger man returned.

Igor didn't pay him any mind. "And I don't know, Vera. Like everything else with Vaslav, it just depends on his mood."

Right.

And maybe the fucking moon, too. Neither of which she could predict.

13.

"Is he really going *everywhere* we go?" Hannah asked. "Even inside?"

Not loudly enough for Kiril to hear at the far end of the pew. Not that Vera thought the older teen would give a shit even if he had heard the question. Something else occupied his mind and hands, the bible he was pretending to read while a blue-eyed, blonde haired girl two rows ahead continued to peek over her shoulder at him.

He acted like he didn't notice.

Vera knew better.

"Everywhere," Vera confirmed.

"But—"

"With the security your mother has paid to tail you for the last year, you'd think you would be used to it by now," she interjected before her friend could complain further. "Besides, I wasn't given a choice about Kiril. He's here whether I want him to be or not."

Hannah pursed her lips. "Yeah, but the security my mother hired didn't look like that."

"I think that's the point. He almost seems harmless."

From a safe distance, maybe.

Until one realized Kiril was terribly quick to anger, wasn't scared of people twice his size, and was damn fast when he needed to be. On his feet and with his fists. She'd seen him take Igor for a round on the grass one evening when the weather was unusually hot for the season, and the two were bored. All good things, as far as Vera was concerned. He could handle himself.

But someone else might not think so.

Hannah lifted her nose a bit at the sight of Kiril, asking, "Or is he just someone to report back about you at the end of the day?"

"Nice, real smooth, Hannah."

Her friend shrugged under her funeral appropriate black dress. Not too tight. A knee length skirt, no cleavage, and the only thing daring about it was the fact Hannah wore the capped sleeve number with only a grey wool shawl wrapped around her for the weather. "I'm just saying—"

"*Shhhh!*"

The hissed shush came from an older woman three pews ahead of theirs in the massive church. The white-haired bird even had the nerve to snap at the two women for their disrespect before she huffed and turned back around in her seat with an armful of furs.

It took seconds before Hannah and Vera broke into a fit of hushed giggles that even drew the attention of Kiril down the way. Thankfully, the rest of the church and service remained uninterrupted by the quiet moment in the very far back.

Vera hadn't realized that Hannah's ex-husband had ties to such a parish that his desecrated remains were allowed to be buried within the walls of the basement crypt. Then again, his family's ties to the Federation were rooted deep going back three generations, so what did Vera know? At least a football field in length, the priest at the front was barely a speck to Vera where he stood at the pulpit.

Kinda creepy.

She didn't like the idea that they were technically walking above dead people. Even if the dead people were special enough to be buried inside, and *under*, the church. Walking through a graveyard made her uncomfortable enough without adding the extra religion, and a few hundred people who regularly attended the church's services on top of the rest like a cherry on a warped sundae.

"Not really the best time for this, is it?" Vera asked her friend when Kiril finally went back to pretending like he was flipping through the Old Testament. He did continue to glance her way every few pages, however.

His message was clear.

Knock it off.

"Yeah, let's not get the puppy barking," Hannah joked.

Loud enough for Kiril to hear. He guffawed back with a middle finger tossed her way, but silently. The two had just enough class, but barely, not to do it right back. And only because the old woman shot them another glaring look over her shoulder.

Vera couldn't tell if the service was almost over or not because neither she nor Hannah had bothered with grabbing one of the programs coming in through the doors. Finding a seat as quickly as possible in the very back had been more important.

Hannah and Vera weren't supposed to draw attention. The only rule of the day the two were expected to follow regarding Viktor's funeral. Not that Hannah was pleased to agree to any rules when she didn't know who was making them ... so to speak.

Or that's how Hannah explained it earlier that morning when Kiril opened the passenger door of his car and delivered the expectations of the day: *It'll be a large service, we're not trying to be looked at, got it?*

"It's *weird*," Hannah muttered.

"What is?"

"A few things, but first, how I feel," her friend said under her breath. Hannah's gaze swept toward Vera behind the black lace covering the upper half of her face, and she tipped her matching floppy brimmed hat in her direction.

The black hats and birdcage veils had been a gift that showed up on Vera's doorstep the night before. Hand delivered by a woman who explained she worked at a specialty boutique in the fashion district, and had received a last-minute call for a very specific order.

Even though Vera fully suspected the morbidly thoughtful gift had come from Vaslav, and he confirmed it when she made a call to him after Hannah went to bed, it made more sense in the morning. Well, after Kiril explained the *rule*.

"I really thought I was going to feel different about today than I do," Hannah admitted, peering out into the aisle and down the pews. Quickly, she fell back into her seat and out of anyone else's view that might be looking. "I don't feel much at all, I guess. I'm numb."

"Except maybe happy for his new wife," Vera said.

She didn't hide the bite in her tone, either.

Hannah nodded. "Yeah, that's true."

Of course, with a funeral that featured well over a few hundred guests scattered amongst a sea of cold, wooden pews ... staying out of the way was a simple task. With the sweeping, heavy curtains framing the balconies overhead, she couldn't even see if there were more people than she initially estimated. In the end, Hannah really hadn't minded being told to stay out of sight. It was Vera's sudden need to be discreet about certain aspects of her life that caused her friend to pick and prod every chance she could.

Vera did well to deflect and excuse her private phone calls and the new, annoying and bossy roommate that came and went from the villa at all hours, but Hannah hadn't let it go on more than a couple of days before she had enough. Vera respected that her friend at least tried to mind her business.

Even if it wasn't for long.

"But more importantly," Hannah said, then, drawing Vera's attention away from the service, "it's weird that my best friend goes out and gets engaged without telling me she did as much to a man she won't even talk to me about. Yeah, that's weird."

Her gaze widened on the last word, and then Hannah nodded to add extra emphasis to her point. As if Vera didn't already understand.

"But is *now* the right time for us to talk about it?" Vera asked again. "Or, no?"

The funeral spoke for itself.

"Why not?" Hannah asked. "What's it matter if it's now or not? The bastard's where he should be … *dead*."

"For somebody who's apparently numb about all this, those are very wet tears," Vera pointed out.

Not unkindly.

Hannah was quick to wipe them away. "I'm glad he's gone."

"Yeah, I know, babe."

Her hand found Hannah's knee over her black skirt, squeezing tight. It helped to settle the sudden sniffles echoing from under her friend's veil. Hannah's constant terror and fear about what Viktor might be planning had disappeared the second a date was posted for his funeral, but being here made it *real*. His need to torment his ex-wife vanished along with his life. Hannah didn't think she needed to keep hiding behind the paid protection offered by her mother which in itself was like stepping into a new life for her friend.

"And I'm worried about you," Hannah said softer. "I used to keep secrets for a dangerous man, too. Once upon a time."

Vera slumped a bit in the pew, chewing on her bottom lip as she considered Hannah's pointed remark. Private and dangerous were the only two words Vera had finally offered Hannah to describe Vaslav the night before as the two women pulled back the blankets on Vera's bed to ready for sleep. All the while Kiril used the spare bedroom with the only other available bed in the villa.

The couch had also been open downstairs. Except she was tired of seeing him sleep on fucking couches.

Vera's conversation with Hannah about Vaslav had

gone on late into the night, whispered into the dark because she honestly didn't think there was a safer time to talk about a man like him than when one couldn't even see a person doing it. Despite the prodding, and Hannah *did* try, Vera was still careful about the details she gave regarding the man she intended to marry.

Instead, she told it like a story.

A broken ballerina who fell in love with a beautiful and sad stranger. She didn't talk about the fact she believed Vaslav was the head of a very large criminal group or that his declining health found him looking for a wife in Vera.

The story had holes.

A lot of them.

Hannah didn't miss even *one*. Never mind that it only took a simple internet search of Vaslav Pashkov's name for unpleasant information to come up in the droves. Searches that Hannah had not so politely shown Vera in the wee hours of the morning.

The thing was, everybody needed a *Hannah* in their life. Someone who noticed the holes in their friend's story and asked the questions that might be uncomfortable. Perhaps if someone had done that very thing with Hannah when her abuse had started with Viktor, things could have been a lot different.

"He's not like Viktor," Vera settled on saying.

"I didn't say—"

"You don't have to, Hannah, but all the same, for what it's worth. He's not."

Hannah folded her arms over her chest, flicking the ends of her shawl in the process and tucking her crystal studded clutch in the crook of her arm. "But is he worse?"

That was a damn good question.

Vera opted not to answer, but not because Hannah didn't deserve one. A group of three men slid one after another out of a pew just a few rows ahead, and one aisle over, from theirs. It was the black suits they wore that Vera noticed first. All tailored, smart and *expensive*. Like the silk underneath each well-fitting blazer. However, when each man left the pew, his hand touched the ball at the back end, carved in wood and stained like the rest.

Tattooed hands.

Rings on the fingers.

A spider on the back.

The group didn't draw attention as they quickly strode down the aisle and out the doors as a commotion from the front drew the rest of the parishioners to their feet. Vera, Hannah, and Kiril stood along with everybody else even though she didn't know why. They certainly hadn't been paying attention to the service, but soon, the low hymn from the congregation buzzed in the air.

The men in black had already passed by their pew. Not one glanced Vera or Hannah's way, but she hadn't missed how her friend noticed the men just like she did.

There was another rule.

One that remained unspoken, but was clear to anyone who had an intimate look at the life of made men. Those who knew of the life didn't speak about it. Things were easier when a person didn't see, hear, or know a thing about the *mafiya*.

"You wanna go?" Vera asked Hannah, then, after she was sure the coast was clear, and they could make a clean exit from the rest of the crowd.

Hannah nodded fast. "Yeah, let's get the hell out of here."

Fine by her.

While the rest of the church continued singing the dead man to the grave, or rather, the crypt, Vera and Hannah slipped out of the pew practically unnoticed. Kiril wasn't too far behind the two, but he didn't offering commentary as he followed along.

"You're still going to go wedding dress shopping with me next week, right?" Vera asked as the two women exited the doors into the main lobby.

Dress shopping was the only thing she could convince Hannah to agree to where the upcoming wedding was concerned. Convinced that Vera was moving too fast, and proclaiming that she hadn't even met Vaslav except for that night under the Eiffel tower, she wouldn't agree to being her friend's official witness.

Yet.

Vera suspected Hannah would give in eventually.

"Who else are you going to take, *him*?" Hannah returned, tossing a look back at Kiril.

"Hey," the kid muttered.

"He'll go, too," Vera admitted.

Hannah scrunched up her freckled face. "But like, outside, right?"

Vera laughed. "For that, probably."

"Well, *good*."

"And I did promise to send pictures to my mom, so you have to be in charge of the camera," Vera added.

Hannah cracked a small smile. "I guess I can handle that, too."

A low hum coming from inside Vera's clutch

stopped the three from exiting the lobby of the church. Vera pulled the phone out, taking it off temporary silence the second she woke up the screen with a click of the power button only to see a text ribbon waiting for her.

From a new phone number that she had yet to punch in a proper contact for. Although, she knew it was Vaslav's most recent phone because he started every text message with the same thing, which usually followed an instruction of some sort. A *call me* or a question in the same vein. Whatever he sent, the first word never changed. Always in English, too, despite the fact he only ever said it to her in Russian.

Kitten.

Phones were just yet another thing Vaslav had too many of. Partly because he often threw them at various other things which meant a device that was supposed to last him weeks before Igor switched it out for a new burner made it through half of what it should before he destroyed it. She couldn't count the *many* phone numbers Vaslav had gone through since that first Paris trip.

Kitten. Don't you know it's rude to leave a funeral before the final procession?—V.

That was all he'd written, and Vera couldn't help but glance over her shoulder the second she had read his words and understood what they meant.

Vas was *there*.

At the funeral.

"Can we get food?" Hannah asked, oblivious to the way Vera quickly stuffed the phone into her clutch. She'd tell Hannah about the text, sure.

Later.

Maybe …

God.

Vera didn't know what she was doing anymore.

"Lunch at the cafe by my place?" Vera offered. "They make the fluffy cakes you like with the almonds."

Hannah peered back through the open doors they had left behind while the rising crescendo of the hymn continued to echo. The place still gave Vera the creeps. "Anywhere, let's just get out of here, okay?"

Kiril stepped in on the girls' conversation, and muttered, "Agreed."

14.

"Kiril is joining the girls for lunch," Igor informed, his voice hushed close behind Vaslav. His head of security had remained standing behind his chair in the private balcony for the better duration of the funeral.

Vaslav had a million better things to do than attend said funeral, and the pieces of the man in the coffin below, centered in front of the altar, certainly wasn't worth his very precious time. In fact, he hadn't planned to be there in the first place which was part of the reason why Viktor's body parts had shown up in garbage bags floating in the canal. He didn't exactly need to make it clear that the death had been a result of the man's *mafiya* dealings when his very discovery spelled the man's end out perfectly clear.

However, Vaslav was also an opportunist. So when an opportunity presented itself, even if it wasn't exactly how he would like for it to arrive, he really had no other option but to take it and run with it. Like today.

"And your ride has arrived out front," Igor added after a brief pause. "The General will be leaving first, and you are to quickly follow."

He didn't bother to ask how Igor could confirm the news. The man's one responsibility when Vaslav was out on and on the move was to make sure his boss could do so safely. While he wasn't always willing to blindly trust Igor, the man *did* know how to do his job.

Particularly well.

Behind the opaque aviator sunglasses that made the light streaming in from the many stained-glass windows slightly more bearable, Vaslav surveyed the lower section of the church long enough to be satisfied that no one down there was looking back at him. The heavy gold drapery framing every balcony from the outside, and around each balcony entrance on the other side, helped with that. At least, the plush, crushed red velvet chairs and thick piled carpeting make the balconies more comfortable for those who were deemed important enough to use them.

Like him.

And his mother.

Unfortunately.

Speaking of which, Vaslav decided his attention was better spent on the people inside the balcony at the moment. Especially because he now needed to slip out without causing unneeded attention and conversation when the funeral wasn't even over.

Essentially, *impossible.*

Which already put Vaslav in a bad mood before he could even rise from his seat. Instead, he took a few seconds to massage the tension and pressure in his forehead and temples. The pain scale teetered somewhere between a too strong seven and a moderate eight. Not quite enough to keep him in bed or bent over a toilet, but enough to wind him when he had to so much as *think*.

Never mind talk.

Yet, time was something Vaslav didn't have at the moment. A fact Igor chose to point out when he said quietly, "Fifteen minutes and the Prosecutor General's limo is leaving, Vas. Before the parish starts to clear out."

"As if it makes any damned difference," he hissed right back.

Wisely, Igor didn't reply.

Why would he?

Vaslav was *right*.

People would still see. *Someone* would recognize the luxury, stretch limo painted black with very specific flags on the front and back waiting at the front of the church, and given how many *vory* from the brotherhood had attended the funeral that day, it was highly unlikely that Vaslav entering said vehicle would also go unnoticed.

A politician, he was not.

"*Vaslav*, honey," came his mother's coo at his left. Vaslav hadn't noticed that Natalia had leaned across the two-foot makeshift aisle between their chairs until she spoke. A great way to put him on an even sharper edge. There was something to be said for the skin-tight dress and blood red claw-like fingernails she opted for the day. The veil that fell around the stiff brim of her black hat didn't hide how glassy her eyes were when he was this close to her face. "You really do need to take the sunglasses off. It's not appropriate."

While he couldn't smell the vodka on her breath, the hot sourness of her words gave it away for him. His previously expressionless face pulled fast into a scowl as he turned to Natalia, and still wouldn't take his sunglasses off.

"*Mat*, you're only here because I needed at least two people from a family to reserve the balcony," Vaslav said. There was something to be said about a church that would sell good seats to anyone with a big enough checkbook, but who was he to judge how priests funded their debauchery and bullshit? Igor didn't count because he was working.

Unfortunately.

Natalia's brows drew together, and anger lit up her gaze. Every word she snapped at him came with spittle and more sour breath. It took him straight back to his chaotic childhood on hard floors with aching bones as she stood above him, *raging*. "Excuse me, *you* invited—"

"Yes, I needed you. One last unfortunate time," he interjected coldly.

Natalia, either too drunk or frustrated that she couldn't get a proper rise out of her son, huffed back into her seat with arms folded over her chest and a childish pout set into her lips. Behind his aviators, Vaslav's gaze narrowed on his mother.

She didn't realize how little he needed her. That she was more of a problem; a thorn in his side that he hadn't been able to remove for years because a part of him was just as human as her. He knew good and well why he was the way he was. A lot of it stemmed from her. Natalia wasn't any different, and he never did see the point in killing a soul that was already dead.

Well, that was then.

"I *despise* you," Vaslav said, making sure every word was clear for his mother to hear despite the fact that he kept his gaze focused on what was ahead of him in the balcony.

Igor cleared his throat behind Vaslav, muttering only, "Ten minutes."

Better make this quick, then.

Natalia's head whipped his way, her gaze widening into fake surprise as she replied, "I feel the same about you, Vas."

Dumb bitch.

She was always so quick to push whatever button of his showed itself. As if it was big, red, and blinking, she couldn't help but slam her entire face into it if it meant Vaslav would bite on the chain she threw at him.

"*Mat*, you're walking on thin ice. You lost what little fondness I had for you the day you put me in the juvenile colony at thirteen. I only kept you alive after I got out of prison because I needed to access the family estate you were pissing away."

"You bastard," Natalia hissed. "You stole that from me."

"Half of it was mine, that's why you really kept me. You needed a child, a boy, for the money and the investment accounts to kick in for you after you spent your own. What were you going to do with the mansion and land in Dubna? You let it rot for *decades*. I only took what was mine."

What she took away from him in the first place.

"And after I had the good grace to provide you with a decent stipend and an apartment you couldn't scoff at," Vaslav continued, "you had the nerve to get me locked up in a madhouse, and then you kept me there for *two fucking years.*"

Slowly, he turned to stare at her, this time pulling his glasses high to sit them on the crown of his head.

"They were going to kill you for what you did. You decapitated a man and delivered his head publicly to his son. In the middle of the day!"

"The bombing really got them worked up, *Mat*, let's be honest."

Vaslav had needed to make choices that day, and not all of them were rational if one didn't live inside his head. Some secrets, he intended to take to his grave.

"Right," she barked out in a sardonic laugh. "You flattened a doctor's office with him inside. I did you a *favor.* They would have executed you in the streets, and danced, you moron." Natalia's gaze burned, and every word she spat between her thin, tight lips felt like knives slicing into his eardrums. "Instead, I paid doctors and lawyers and everyone else you needed to say you were crazy, *and they did it!* Because of me!"

The sound of feet shuffling as the parishioners stood for what would be the final hymn, according to a stoic Igor still behind him, muffled his mother's shout. *Barely.*

Vaslav chuckled, scratching through his coarse facial hair with fingers he'd rather use to wrap around Natalia's throat. "You forgot the part where you did all of that with money you funded and pilfered from my accounts. Or when you paid the institution more of *my money*, again, to keep me locked away for longer. You were having the time of your life, *Mat.*"

On his dime, and while he went insane, heartbroken, and entirely alone, and she wanted praise for that? *Gratitude?*

What really was insanity?

If not for Igor, and rest his soul, Nico, the brotherhood would have crumbled. They kept every brigadier in line and stayed loyal to a man they could only talk to through smuggled letters written on stolen paper. Ink, however, could be made from various things.

Fun times.

"*Five* minutes," Igor prodded with a bit more sternness.

Right, back to the matter at hand.

He didn't even mention to his mother that the call she made to her illegitimate brother hadn't exactly ended with the promise of a dinner. Natalia had no clue why Vaslav actually wanted to attend the funeral, but the Antonovich family name was just important enough for her to agree to put on a black dress and grief veil for a day. Her vanity, and an ever-present need to social climb despite her mid-sixties fast approaching, encouraged her to quickly agree to whatever he proposed.

On the other hand, the parking lot was the perfect no-man's land for a well-known criminal, and said criminal's politically influential uncle to meet with justifiable reasoning if they had both attended the same event.

Or rather, if it appeared like they did.

Appearance was everything, after all.

"Why is it that every time the two of us are in a room together," Natalia started with the cock of one perfectly manicured eyebrow, and a wag of a finger between their respective seats, "we end up doing this? We could just ... *not* be near one another, no?"

Vaslav smirked and nodded. "I agree."

Starting now.

"What are you doing?" Natalia asked, her voice pitching high. "Where are you going?"

Vaslav stood, adjusting his blazer in the front as he did so. "I have things to do, and your usefulness ran out about five minutes ago, so none of those things include you. But back to what matters."

"Excuse me?" she questioned with the same air of indignance.

It took practically no time at all for him to become bored with her *poor pity me, the victim* act. "Your allowance ended as of your last payment, and your building dues are paid up until the end of the month. My financial help ends then, *Mat*. I can't imagine how you're going to keep the hotel suites you've been switching out every week or so since I added that extra on top every month, but that also isn't my problem. Hopefully the amount of my money you poured into all that plastic surgery will still make you worth something to the names in your black book, hmm?"

"You *prick*!"

"Get a new insult. That only hurt when I was a boy." Vaslav smiled down at his mother. "Also, the gate to the property in Dubna will no longer be open to you, and trespassers are shot on sight."

Natalia gasped, indignant in a blink. "You wouldn't, Vaslav."

"*Mat*, I will personally pull the trigger and dig your grave."

The hymn down below finally ended.

Vaslav had *maybe* two minutes to catch his ride outside.

"And if you think you want to challenge me in

court or elsewhere, if there's even an ounce in you that believes there's anything left for you to take, *Mat*," Vaslav informed with a shrug of his shoulders as he turned to follow an already retreating Igor from the private balcony, "I hate to tell, but don't waste your breath. As of the first of December, my new wife will gain ownership of every account, property, investment, and anything else in my name that's there for her to have."

"*Married?*" she shrieked as a realization dawned over her face. "That's … less than thirty days away!"

It was entirely possible that someone down below might have heard her with the priest's murmurings echoing through the old church's speaker system. Vaslav simply didn't care.

"Yes, and not enough time for you to put any kind of plan together," Vaslav said as he headed down the aisle in the small balcony between the rows of chairs. Only four, with two chairs on either side. "Have a lonely trip to hell, *Mat*."

"Vaslav! Where are you going? We are not done speaking here! *Vaslav!*"

And may she forever rot there.

Igor waited in the corridor outside the balcony for Vaslav to pass before he followed right behind, saying, "While we're in the city, we could make a trip downtown. Your accountant has the money ready."

"It only took him two fucking months."

Which was the only reason why Vaslav didn't make a trip to Feliks' beloved Swan House after he left a reminder in the form of a written note on Vera's front door. He disliked the idea that Feliks had unfortunately tied Vera to Vaslav in a way that meant she could be a messenger for him.

That would end.

Soon.

Igor sniffed, muttering, "Nobody has a hundred million in American dollars on hand, Vas."

Fair enough.

The bigger question at hand?

"Had it been a check, or even a transfer, Feliks could have had his money a lot sooner," Vaslav told Igor. Unlike others who didn't have a significant amount of money on hand, Vaslav did. In various accounts from banks all across the world. He never kept more than a handful of millions in one account in case it was flagged or closed for some reason.

It still took time to turn digital into paper.

"His business is failing, his life is practically over," Vaslav said more to himself than Igor, "and Feliks didn't want instant money. Essentially."

His man didn't reply.

Vaslav didn't need him to.

"No, not Feliks," Vaslav muttered, still working over the problem at hand in his mind, turning the corner at the end of the hall that led to a stairwell. "Feliks wants *cash.*"

"Apparently," Igor returned, "it took six duffle bags to hold it all, too."

Of course, it did.

*

Igor exited the church behind Vaslav, but didn't say a word as his boss took the grand stairs at the front two at a time. The taillights of a Mercedes limo pulling away from the curb came on to signal the driver inside had hit the brakes before he could pull out onto the street. When the vehicle stayed put, Vaslav trusted that the man waiting inside was willing to give him the grace of an extra couple of minutes.

He appreciated it.

Nobody liked tardiness as a valued trait.

The flapping flags on all four points of the limo reflected the Russian Federation, and while the steps were mostly clear of loiterers, he tried not to be the only person that lingered. The less eyes that watched him exit the church and enter his uncle's limo, the better. He *hated* when people talked. It required work to shut them up.

Who really had the time?

"I won't be far behind, boss," Igor called from behind.

Vaslav replied with a two-finger wave over his shoulder as he reached the bottom of the stairs, but as he reached the parked limo and came up along the back door, he paused with a glance back at Igor. "Lunch, yeah?"

Behind his own dark sunglasses, Igor's brow lifted high. "Pardon?"

"The girls, and Kiril. Lunch?"

"Yeah, at the cafe near her villa. The one she likes."

"Good, I could eat," Vaslav returned.

"With a migraine?" Igor asked carefully.

"I said *could*, not would."

And eating wasn't really the point.

Vaslav left Igor alone to figure out his intentions without further explanation. Opening the limo and slipping inside without as much as glancing around to see if there was anyone watching, he let the door quickly slam shut behind him. As soon as he was inside the dimly lit rear of the vehicle, he found the closest place to sit.

One of the white leather bench seats. Pulling the aviators from his face to dig his fingers in good to his eye sockets just long enough to relieve some of the pressure, it took a few seconds longer for his vision to clear up once he pulled his hand away.

Only to see a smiling, familiar face.

Vaslav did not smile back.

"I hear congratulations are in order," his uncle, Dimitry, said. "Igor explained you had intentions on getting married in a few weeks. I hope you don't plan on sending me an invitation, *plemyannik, nephew*. I'd hate to refuse."

Then, the man at the back end of the limo chuckled, still smiling as he said, "No offence, of course."

None taken.

Vaslav waved it off between them, and the similarities between the two did not go unnoticed to him. The physical ones, that was. From the strong facial bone structure to the same ice-blue gaze. While his uncle had at least thirty or forty pounds of girth to him that Vaslav had managed to stave off in his age, Dimitry was still tall, broad-shouldered, and a significant presence in any room.

If not for knowing he had taken after his grandfather, Dimitry's biological father, he might have thought the man across from him had done the deed with his mother to produce him. Thankfully, their family secrets didn't run *that* deep.

Nonetheless it never had, not even when he was a fifteen-year-old thug in a juvenile colony facing more time in an adult establishment that would treat him much less kindly, and his uncle visited him one last time. It was the sight of Dimitry in a three-piece suit with glittering gold rings on every finger on the other side of cracked cement and bars while Vaslav wore prison scraps and had to be shackled to the floor that day long ago that taught him about the kind of criminal he wanted to be. It wasn't the kind that sat where he did.

Vaslav learned a lot in the span of his fifteen-year incarceration. Specifically, that he didn't intend on going back. *Ever.*

"*Good behavior will get you out of this situation a lot faster, nephew,*" Dimitry had told him that day.

All the while, Vaslav had been suffering from a terribly bruised and swollen face that made talking difficult. Compliments of the illegal fighting between the incarcerated youth; fights that the guards organized to keep entertained. At least it taught him how to *really* survive.

"*Da,*" he remembered agreeing with his uncle, and then he quickly followed it up with a simple, "*but good behavior isn't going to keep me alive in here.*"

"I heard you need another mess sorted out," Dimitry said, bringing Vaslav back to the present issue at hand. The only reason the two had needed this conversation to happen in the first place.

The limo had long since pulled away from the curb, but Vaslav didn't care to see what streets the driver took them down as long as Igor trailed behind.

"Ask your driver where my man is," Vaslav said.

Dimitry cocked a brow at the request and reached over to press a button on the middle console of his own bucket seat. A dark screen slid to the side with a buzz next to Vaslav's head, and he turned just enough to see the man positioned on the other side, manning the limo.

"Is there an SUV behind us?" Dimitry asked.

"A black one."

His uncle looked at him, then. "Satisfied?"

Vaslav shrugged. "Barely."

A tight smile answered that response. "I didn't expect anything less." Dimitry hit the button again, and the screen closed as fast as it had opened. "If you talk at a moderate level, he can't make out what you're saying."

Vaslav wished he cared about what his uncle's driver heard. No doubt, the man was paid handsomely to hear nothing at all.

"What did Bogdan have to say?" Dimitry asked as the limo took a turn too fast for Vaslav's comfort.

"Jesus, where'd he learn to drive?"

Dimitry never missed a beat. "Vaslav, if we're going to talk about the bodies in the canal, then I'm going to at least need an interesting conversation beforehand."

"You only know about my fucking head doctor—"

"It's a harmless curiosity, Bogdan is a friend, and if not for me, he wouldn't have looked twice at your case. And give the man a little respect, he's not a *head* doctor. He's a—"

"I know what he is," Vaslav snapped back.

Dimitry rolled his eyes, the only show of his irritation before he focused his attention on the scenery passing them by beyond his tinted window. "It's not good, is it?"

Good God.

Vaslav did not have time for this. "Ten or so good years with a cocktail of medication, clinical monitoring, and other required things that I just can't produce at the moment."

"*Good* years, what does that mean?"

To Vaslav?

"What's left that's worth to live," he muttered.

He was allowed the right to say it. It was *his* life, after all. Even the end of it.

"What is it, the dementia?"

Unsurprising that Dimitry went there first. That's what had eventually wasted away his own father while Natalia pissed away the family fortune.

Vaslav sighed, scowling at the man across the limo because Dimitry couldn't just drop it. It didn't help that he understood the only reason his uncle pressed was because the man cared. Oh, he might not welcome public attachment or communication to his nephew in any way, but throughout his life, Dimitry had been there when no one asked him to be.

Especially Vaslav.

"It doesn't matter what it is," Vaslav settled on saying. "It's *there*."

And it would eventually kill him. One way or another.

"Right, well, that's unfortunate, no?"

Vaslav's scowl deepened further. "I'm dealing with it."

Nobody said he had to deal with it well.

"It's far easier to overlook and explain away bodies washing up in the canal when they aren't bodies of people you have known contact with," Dimitry noted, "not to mention, if they didn't keep showing up in rubbish bags."

"The trash bags help with the mess, or so Igor says," Vaslav replied.

Dimitry glanced his way, then, unimpressed. "But

not with the public speculation, hmm?"

Vaslav didn't bother to point out the amount of money he had shelled out to officers and other officials across the city to quietly and swiftly move on from his … *messes*. No doubt, Dimitry already had a full scope, given his own reach inside the institution.

"I don't want to ever see my name in the papers again," Vaslav said. "I'm not asking for much."

"Yet, you keep killing people. Do you see how those two things don't fit together?"

"Wouldn't have to do the killing bit, either, if said people would stay out of my business and follow the fucking rules."

It wasn't hard.

Dimitry nodded once, and then his gaze landed on Vaslav. With a good quarter of a century between the two in age, it was the life experience and power his uncle had achieved that lended to the respect Vaslav offered the man.

Very little else.

Blood counted for almost nothing, now.

"This is the last time I am cleaning up one of your messes," Dimitry warned. "I better not hear of one more body floating up in the canal."

"I've already figured out a new way to handle that problem. Worry not."

Dimitry's pursed lips told Vaslav that the man wasn't happy with his nephew's reply. "Frankly, I'd rather not know, and one more thing, *da*?"

"Yes, what?"

"Make sure your fucking mother never calls me again, or else the last thing you ever want to do is ask me for one more favor, Vaslav. Mark my words."

Fair enough.

"You never answer when I call," Vaslav said.

"I sincerely hope you don't wonder *why*."

Vaslav didn't wonder. A call from him meant nothing good.

Chuckling under his breath, he muttered, "Natalia isn't a real concern. After this month, she won't even have a penny to pay for the phone she called you from."

Dimitry didn't ask for details.

Natalia wasn't that important, honestly.

"Back to the church, then?" Dimitry asked. "Is that where you'd like to go?"

"No, actually," Vaslav replied. "How would your driver feel about taking me a dozen blocks east?"

Dimitry, letting out an annoyed grunt, reached over to press the button the console to his left once more. "Why the hell not? You've already wasted half of my day. Let's add another hour to the clock. I clearly don't have anything better to do."

He said it, not Vaslav.

15.

Vera glanced between the chicken sandwich on rye bread and the Almond Puff sitting right beside it on another plate. She could already taste the flaky sweetness that would soon melt in her mouth. The small, tucked away cafe really did have a knack for homemade, fresh-baked cakes and pastries.

Hannah's choice in lunch matched Vera's right down to the vanilla chai lattes in little pink mugs. Each featured hand painted matryoshkas along the outside upper rim. Between the four plates and two mugs, there wasn't much more room on the small round table, and there had only been seats for two. Kiril ended up three tables down.

Not that it mattered.

The cafe was mostly empty other than a boy, maybe eleven, or twelve, and who Vera suspected might be his little brother sitting across from him in the booth. The two boys sat opposite to Kiril who barely glanced up from whatever he was scrolling through on his phone.

A line of booths faced the front windows of the cafe, converted from the ground floor of an old bookmaker's shop. Old tools and bindings hung displayed from bare rafters.

Their trio was lucky to arrive just after the afternoon rush that typically kept the cafe full and buzzing with activity. Vera waved her fork at the two plates closer to her, asking Hannah, "You wouldn't judge me for eating dessert first, right?"

The freckles splattered across Hannah's face almost seemed to dance with the same happiness as her eyes when she laughed. "That was my plan, too."

Hannah picked up the tiny three-pronged fork that had come with her Almond Puff, and stabbed it into the corner of the rectangular chunk of sugary heaven, promptly plopping the bite into her mouth. Winking and nodding as she chewed, Hannah didn't need to talk for Vera to understand.

Melt-in-your-mouth goodness.

She was half way through her own pastry, making an effort not to moan around every thin slice of crunchy almond that made up the top layer of the puff; her favorite part of the sweet. The buzz of Vera's phone in the clutch she'd hung off the corner of the chair broke the silence between the two. Hannah shot her a questioning look.

"It's a bit early for your mom or dad to be texting you from New York, right?" Then, she squinted one eye, asking, "Or am I off on the time zones? Didn't you get a message when we were leaving the church, too?"

"Just ask me who's messaging me," Vera told her friend. "We can skip the twenty questions."

Hannah pouted exaggeratedly. "You're no fun."

"You're *nosy*."

With a shrug, Hannah didn't deny it. She did, however, say quietly, "Only maybe a little worried, too."

Vera used the phone she pulled out of her clutch as a momentary distraction from the conversation. She didn't think it would stop Hannah from bringing it up again, however. While her friend lifted her mug for a sip of latte, Vera checked her phone for the cause of the buzzing alert.

A smile bloomed instantly. "The invitations are ready."

Hannah's brow lifted high as she lowered the mug back to the table. "That was fast. Didn't you put the order in two days ago?"

Vera shrugged. "I only needed ten, and they didn't have to be … *fancy*, or anything."

Not to mention, the invitations didn't need very much information. Her name, Vaslav's, too. A standard greeting and appropriate invite followed by a time and an address to a church in Dubna that Vera had yet to visit. It had been, however, requested by Vaslav for reasons he promised to explain later.

"You're really only inviting *ten* people?" Hannah asked.

Vera nodded. "Who else needs one?"

"I can name twenty women off the top of my head who would appreciate an invitation from you to literally *anything*." Hannah yanked her chicken sandwich plate closer and picked up one triangular half in both hands. "And I know you have more family than your parents, so. Say it like it is. Vaslav Pashkov said ten guests, and ten it is."

Vera barely suppressed a smile. "Getting right to the point, are you?"

Hannah sighed and stared at her sandwich like she might take a bite. Instead, she told Vera first, "You know he spent time in an institution, right? Not just *prison* institutions, Vera."

"I saw the newspaper records you found on the online archives."

Yet another thing Hannah had tried to bring to Vera's attention over the past evenings. She simply hadn't read through them as carefully as maybe she should have, except the information felt like an invasion of Vaslav's privacy, in a way.

"He did terrible things to people," Hannah said, "and it doesn't take very much to find what those things were, either."

He still does, Vera almost said.

Hannah had no fucking clue.

Instead of speaking what was on her mind, because she loved her friend just enough to put up with her prodding and concerns as it came from a good place, Vera glanced back down at her phone. She smiled at the image the designer and printer had attached of the simple and elegant invitations printed on cream card stock, framed by flaked gold leaf with black script in the middle spelling out her name and Vaslav's larger than the rest of the writing.

She was lucky to have a contact at a printer in the city who could get the invitations done as fast as they had; one of the only good things she had gained from The Swan House.

The guy used to do all their promo, promised to be discreet, and fast. All of which he had been, so far. Vera appreciated it.

THE BEAUTY WHO LOVED HIM

"I really wanted to be able to get one sent to my parents—*properly*, in the mail," Vera added, shooting Hannah a look, "before the actual wedding happens."

Hannah laughed. "Better get it in the mail, then."

That was the plan.

"I bet we could get Kiril to run us over to the printer to pick them up," Vera said.

Hannah, chewing through another bite in her sandwich, eyed Vera as she finished the bite. All the while, the crease of tension in her friend's forehead softened with every chew. Eventually, she swallowed the food, and muttered, "Just say it, Vera."

"Say what?"

"You're excited."

Vera sucked in a breath, holding it in her chest as she wondered; *is that what this is?* The humming she felt in her chest, and the butterflies in her belly? The urge to look at her phone, and the image on the text again to see her name below his on cream card stock was that all just excitement? The wedding only a handful of weeks away was the first step to an uncertain future, but that didn't stop her from looking forward to it all the same.

"It's more than that, too," Vera said, letting that breath she'd been holding out. "But he's private, for *good* reason, and I don't mind following along with his wishes if it means he's comfortable. And just so you know, one of these invitations" —she waved her phone— "is for you."

"*Obviously*, I'd be mad if one wasn't," Hannah threw back, sending both women into a fit of hushed giggles.

Eventually, Vera calmed enough to ask, "But you still won't be my legal witness?"

Hannah eyed the quiet street outside the cafe from the wall of bay windows overlooking the scene. "Just to be clear, you getting married won't change anything about you and me, right?"

"Of course, not."

Hannah's head bobbed up and down once. "I guess I better do it, huh?"

Vera only grinned. "We can pick a dress for you next week, too."

"Are you paying?"

Like Hannah didn't have the money, but all the same ...

"No, actually," Vera said, smirking while she put the phone away. "Vaslav is."

*

Vera, halfway through her chicken sandwich while Hannah took a minute in the bathroom at the far end of the cafe, was lost devouring her lunch until Kiril swept past her in the aisle. She barely had the chance to look up and see him go before she heard the familiar *ting* of the bell over the cafe's front door. She turned around in her seat as he exited the cafe at the same time a black limo came to a stop on the side of the street.

The unusual vehicle, with flags flapping from what she could see from the front, didn't linger long. The second a figure dressed in black stepped out of the rear and closed the door, the limo pulled back onto the road as if it hadn't even been in park.

A black SUV took its place.

One she recognized.

Vera didn't pay Igor's arriving SUV much mind

because she was more interested in the figure that exited the street to enter the cafe. Vaslav was a hell of a sight for sore eyes when he decided to make a public debut. Of course, she'd witnessed him smartly dressed in a three-piece suit with a well-fitted blazer and vest and tie that matched the silk of his pocket square, all deep red. It didn't change how the presence of him walking toward her from behind with purpose could practically shrink the entire world around her.

Swinging around in her seat at the same time Vaslav took the open chair across from hers, *Hannah's*, all she could ask the man hiding his eyes behind dark aviators was, "What are you doing here?"

Vaslav smiled, or *tried*. His lips didn't quite pull high enough for a full smile and fell too quickly. "Didn't I promise you a date?"

"I thought I needed a black dress for the date?"

His chin tilted higher, and while she couldn't see his eyes behind the opaque lenses, she could feel the way he stared at the dress hugging her curves. "Looks like you're wearing black to me."

"You said to buy a *new* dress."

"Did I?"

He even had the nerve to cock a brow.

Vera refused to play his word game. "Just say you were at the funeral today, and Kiril probably passed along the message where we were going for lunch."

"Conversations are less fun that way," Vaslav returned.

She didn't get the chance to reply because Kiril swept past the table again to return to his own with a wave. The man who followed behind the teenager, however, stopped at their table. Also dressed in a black three-piece suit, although his shirt, vest and tie underneath were the same dark hue, Igor folded his hands at his back and cleared his throat.

Vaslav didn't look away from Vera. She, on the other hand, stared up at Igor.

"You good?" Igor asked.

Vaslav shrugged, asking Vera, "Are you?"

What did the question have anything to do with her?

"Why wouldn't I be?"

The man across the table tipped his head toward Igor, saying only, "We're fine."

"I could run over to pick up the bags, save us the trouble later, no?"

Vera had clearly missed something in the conversation, but the two continued with their back and forth as if she hadn't even been brought into it in the first place.

"The pup is right there," Vaslav said with a gesture toward the quiet teenager a couple of tables away. "I'm sure he can manage."

"Next time," Igor drawled out as he turned to walk away, giving Vera a wink as he went, "just let me know we're going for lunch."

Vaslav graced the retreating man with an annoyed wave, and loudly muttered, "I thought you had figured it out!"

"Are you?" Vera asked him, then.

Vaslav pushed his aviator's high on the crown of his head, and the hard squint of his brow gave away the truth; his pain. "Am I what?"

"Having lunch?"

"Not sure I can keep down what I might eat, but I knew I could get a few minutes with you." As he spoke, Vaslav reached across the table for her. Vera couldn't stop herself from letting her hands slip into his over the plates between them. He twisted her large engagement ring between two fingers before flipping over her hand, palm up, and kissed every one of her fingertips. As unexpected as it was sweet, she was helpless to let him do it while she melted from the inside. "Even if it's not a proper date, *kisska*," he said.

Oh, she figured.

Vera didn't mind, to be honest. She'd take a few minutes with him over food, too.

"Good," came a familiar voice, but new to the conversation. "I really hate being a third wheel."

Heat flushed through Vera's whole body. Vaslav even chuckled at the sight of her blush creeping over her grinning cheeks at being interrupted by her friend, the bastard. She hadn't heard Hannah's approach from behind until she spoke.

"Ah," Vaslav said, turning his pain-riddled scowl on Hannah as she moved to stand beside their table instead of behind Vera. "The *friend*. Hannah, is it?"

He even stuck out his hand for a shake.

Hannah never once broke Vaslav's gaze as she lightly shook his hand, her red ringlets bouncing as she fixed him with a hard stare. "It is. Hannah Malone. Don't bother with your name, I already know it. And you're in my seat."

That earned her a smirk.

Only a little one.

Vaslav let go of Hannah's hand, saying at the same time, "Well, I'll get you another."

Too amused to step in and stop the two from sniping at one another like they were, Vera remained quiet as Vaslav learned across the aisle and grabbed an empty chair from a table beside theirs. Hannah's plates were all but empty, so it wasn't exactly like they needed the table space for a third seat. Vaslav yanked the wooden chair around to face their table, and nodded at it, telling Hannah, "There, *sit*."

His tone stayed clipped.

Short, and annoyed.

She did sit.

Quickly, too.

"If you call me "*the friend*" again," Hannah told Vaslav, arching one red eyebrow high, "I'll start calling you the fiancé in kind. Fair?"

Of all things she could have said, that remark actually earned Hannah a smile. Softer than his smirks and fleeting because of his pain. It had been there, though. For a second.

"Fair," Vaslav said.

"Well," Vera put in, waving for the server behind the breakfast bar made of centuries old wood, "this wasn't awkward *at all*."

Then, she looked to Vas, asking, "Do you want a coffee?"

"Black, please," he muttered.

By the time Vera had repeated the order to a waiting server, the other two people at the table had attempted a restart to their conversation.

Kind of.

"You are aware that the general public basically believes you're not allowed to leave Dubna, aren't you?" Hannah asked. "Like you've got some kind of gate and guard out there keeping you behind lock and key."

"*Hannah*," Vera scolded, interjecting into the conversation fast. "That's—"

Vaslav laughed, guttural and *real*. It stopped her from saying anything else to shut her friend up before the unpredictable nature of the man sitting at the table decided to show itself at the worst possible time.

Except he didn't react like she expected.

It shocked even Vera.

"Jesus Christ," Vaslav swore, rubbing at his cheek as he turned away from the table a bit. "The papers really will write anything, yeah?"

Hannah shot Vera a pointed look, with a flat, "And some of it might even be true."

"Thin ice," Vera replied dryly. "You're walking on it."

"Oh, she's harmless," Vaslav said, stunning Vera further. "And funny, I like her."

Not even Hannah knew what to make of that.

16.

When the first snow fell in Moscow, Vera swore the city changed. All the color and cement and life turned into a beautiful palace of ice. Every street and block, and even business, looked different with snow clinging to the roofs and ice hanging from the eaves. While they only had a couple of weeks of terribly cold temperatures most winters, from the first snowfall to the last in April, the weather remained mild.

The first snowfall of the year came right on time, too. Early November greeted them with the same chill and wind it always did, but Vera could have done without needing to wear a thick parka complete with a fur-trimmed hood on the day she went shopping for wedding dresses. The falling snow with every large flake spiraling down in the winds was certainly beautiful, and it meant she was one day closer to her wedding day, but shopping downtown was a hell of a lot less fun in the cold.

The quiet whistle of appreciation from Claire as her

mother observed the beginnings of the city's first winter storm made Vera even happier that she was safely inside. Turning the tablet back around so Claire could see her daughter's face instead of the bay window where the boutique's private dressing room overlooked the icy, but still slightly busy, street.

"I hope you're not walking home," Claire joked.

Vera grinned, replying, "Definitely not."

Her mother didn't notice the way Vera's attention drifted off screen to something outside the windows. Or rather, *someone*. Kiril sat parked in the SUV that Igor had dropped off for him to use that morning. Not that he was entirely pleased with the idea, even if the vehicle did feature studded winter tires and more traction compared to his sporty coupe.

He'd pouted the whole way into the city. Vera bet he'd do the same thing the entire way home, too. At least, she and Hannah both had the good sense to be grateful for the change in vehicle. And the extra room.

"But back to what *really* matters," Claire said as Vera turned to head back across the freshly waxed hardwood floors to where Hannah waited on the leather couch. "Which is, which dress did you pick? The one you're wearing or the first you tried?"

"She's not going to tell us," Hannah spoke up.

Vera stuck her tongue out at her friend. "You don't know that."

"Yes, I do. I bet you'll want to keep it special. *Secret.*"

Well …

Why did Hannah have to know her so well? Really, she only planned to keep it a secret from two people. Each for their own special reasons.

Hannah reached for the tablet then, waving for Vera to give it to her until she did. Looking right in the face of Vera's mother, Hannah told her unabashedly, "But I can show you what she plans to wear underneath it."

"*Hannah!*"

Vera's shriek went unheeded in her friend's peeling giggles. She didn't make a move to do what she promised, although it didn't appear like Claire minded the filthy joke what with the way her laughter echoed from the tablet.

The thing was, Hannah could follow through.

Three boxes, all topped with red lace ribbons, rested on the glass top of the coffee table in front of the sofa where Hannah sat. Each box, which had been waiting for her with a note that they had been chosen for her to try, featured a lace panty and bra set. All in various styles. Thong. Bikini. High-waisted. Every set had a matching pair of stockings. Each in a different color.

White.

Black.

Red.

Vera didn't know how Vaslav managed to get his hand in just about every aspect of her life, but he did so in such a way that it hadn't bothered her. *Too much.* So, she let him get away with it. Not that she seriously believed if she told him to knock it off, that he would.

"Oh, it doesn't matter, I know which dress she's going to pick," Vera heard her mother say as she turned to face the wall of mirrors opposite to the sofa.

"Oh?"

"Yeah," Vera said before her mother could reply to

Hannah, "the one I'm wearing."

The two mirrors in the very middle acted as the doors that opened to a single, moderately sized private dressing room featuring more mirrors, and a similar white leather chair and stool, but were currently closed.

Vera admired the way the last dress she'd tried on clung to every dip and curve of her body. Mostly silk, the bodice of the gown clung low on her breasts, and the only sleeves were two limp bands of silk that fell down her shoulders. She was drawn to the way the low cut put her throat and shoulders on display.

While there was a bit more skirt to the dress than she initially thought she would go for, there was something about the way the cinched waist opened a bit at her hips that made her curves even more apparent. The back of the silk skirt fell heavily to the floor with a good foot of train. Just enough to make the skirt billow. A band of delicate lace trimmed the very edge of the skirt's hem. Similar enough to the lace of the veil that had once been intended for her biological mother, the choice in dress was easy.

Hannah was just slow to figure it out.

Vera didn't need to try on another dress after the last one she'd put on because the second she slipped the pearl white silk over her head, *she knew*. It was perfect.

Every inch.

Understated.

Classic.

Her.

"You know that one comes in blush *and* black," Hannah put in while Vera continued admiring her reflection.

She considered the black option.

Only for a second.

"I'm not dyeing Gia's veil," Vera said.

"Good choice, your father might puke," Claire muttered in a low laugh.

At the mention of her father, Vera swung around to say, "And don't you dare give him even a hint about what my dress looks like, Ma."

Hannah, sweet as could be, turned the tablet around for Vera to see her mother still in the process of rolling her eyes.

"How little faith you have in me," Claire returned.

She wanted to deny her mother's claim, but the sight of herself still draped in beautiful, heavy white silk was impossible to ignore. Almost surreal.

"This is really happening," Vera whispered.

Apparently, not low enough for the other people in the space to hear—virtually, and otherwise.

"I remember that feeling," Claire mused.

"Me, too," Hannah muttered, "but then the bastard had to go and ruin it."

17.

"Hello, *kisska.*"

Vera clung tighter to the phone like it might bring her closer to the man who answered on the other end. "Vas."

"Aren't you shopping for dresses? Why on earth are you calling me?"

A valid question. Even if he did ask it impatiently.

Vera didn't typically call Vaslav without his prompting through a text first because that's what he preferred. He didn't pretend to like talking on the phone, and she didn't push him on it considering he was easier to appreciate when he was less annoyed.

Mostly.

"You know I love you, don't you?"

Vaslav paused on the question before asking, "What does that have anything to do with dress shopping?"

"Well, nothing. Sort of," Vera added quickly. "But then I—"

"Are you dress shopping?" he injected, *demanding*.

"Yes! I'm sitting in the dressing room right now."

"Send me a picture."

Vera's brow jumped high. "Excuse me?"

"A picture. With your phone. *Send it.*"

"What if I was wearing my dress?"

"Are you?" he returned.

"Stop talking me in circles," Vera returned. "That's not the point, and you know it."

She didn't have any intention of explaining that she had already picked her dress, paid for it with the card Vaslav had provided, and Hannah was currently browsing for an appropriate gown herself. That wasn't even why she'd decided to call him.

"You would have come right out with that, *kisska*, if you were wearing something you didn't want me to see." She surmised he was at home, but other than the sound of footsteps, she couldn't hear anything else on the other end of the phone. "Send me a picture, or I call Kiril and ask him where you are."

"You really don't believe me?"

"Trust is a ... *tricky* thing," Vaslav muttered.

No, he was just a very complicated man. She had figured that detail out before agreeing to marrying him, and had accepted it was a part of the package that made up the man who had unintentionally captured her heart.

"Don't call Kiril," Vera grumbled. "He'll come inside and make a damn scene."

Just because he was probably bored by now.

"Then send a picture."

Vera rolled her eyes. "Give me a second ... impatience helps no one."

"And yet, impatience somehow gets me

everywhere."

Frankly, she didn't mind playing along with Vaslav's game because she intended for him to eat his words. Or rather, his request. He couldn't possibly know that even though she'd finished her dress shopping, including finding a black number for a possible date that may or may not happen, she had decided to try on the sets of lingerie.

Well, one set of three. The set she couldn't wear on the wedding day because the straps of the bra weren't removable.

Vera didn't bother to stand from the white leather chair in the middle of the changing room to take the picture of her reflection in the wall of mirrors. She didn't need to. With her legs crossed, she'd propped her elbow up on the armrest of the chair to get a good, steady shot of her body's profile wrapped in stark red lace. She even winked for the picture, too.

All the while, Vaslav remained quiet on the phone. She knew when her picture text had been sent through, and he pulled the photo up, because he didn't try to hide the grunt that proceeded the clearing of his throat.

"*Damn*," he praised.

Vera smiled.

Only to herself.

"See, I am in the changing room as we speak," she said.

Vaslav's responding sigh came out breathy and terse. "Did you try on the other two as well?"

"They're the same size, so I don't really need to. They'll fit, and I'd like to keep them perfect until the wedding, you know?"

She didn't explain why she opted to try on the red

set. That would give Vaslav too much information to go on regarding her dress and what it might look like. Not that he asked.

Yet.

"Good, save the white set so I can ruin it first, and the black set for the night after."

Vera eyed her reflection as she toyed with the red strap of the lace bra. "That's why I called, actually."

"Pardon?"

"The lingerie," she clarified. "I wanted to tell you they're good choices."

"*Da*, for anything. Including taking them off. And speaking of things getting off, how about you? *Now.*"

Vera stilled in the chair, unsure that she'd heard him right. "You're not serious?"

"As a fucking heart attack. You should not have sent me that picture if you didn't intend to make it worth my while, beautiful. Can someone see you?"

"No," Vera assured.

"*Hear* you?"

Did he hear her swallow just then?

"Maybe," she admitted, less sure.

The walls of the private dressing room weren't particularly thick. Yes, Hannah was down shopping on the main floor of the private boutique known affectionately as the *Dollhouse* by the ladies running the place. Vera probably wouldn't be interrupted for a while, either.

"Be *very* quiet, yes," Vaslav murmured.

"Vas—"

"But make good and sure I can hear you, *kisska.*"

Oh, God.

It was hard to deny him when his voice sounded almost like a purr against her cheek through the speaker of the phone. All it took was closing her eyes, and Vera could imagine him there. The friction of him stepping between her widening knees. The way he'd touch her without abandon, leaving no piece of her body unloved by his attention. She could even smell him, *taste him*, too, if she tried hard enough. The thing was, even the memory of him was enough to get her body limboing in a hellish place.

Somewhere between want and need but feeding the urges wouldn't necessarily give her precisely what her body craved—*him*.

Like muscle memory, he'd imprinted himself there, sure—in her mind, rushing through her veins. All over. She couldn't forget the way he'd made her feel at one point or another.

He was there.

Even when he wasn't.

She couldn't hide the shakiness in her next exhale.

Vaslav didn't miss it, either.

"You want to," he said with a taunting flair. "I bet your hand is already between your thighs or damn close. Are you wet?"

Vera laughed weakly. "My hand is *not*—"

"How close is it?"

She wet the seam of her lips with her tongue, whispering, "One is holding the phone, thank you."

"And the other?"

This man.

"On the armrest of the chair, Vaslav," Vera said, refusing to give into his tempting game. "I'm supposed to go help Hannah pick a dress. I am *not* sitting here masturbating on the phone for you."

"You haven't even thought about moving off that chair, have you?" he asked, confident. "Between the two of us, let's get fucking real."

And *cocky*.

"Vas—"

"I haven't touched you in more days than I care to count, so the very least you could do is let me hear you pretend like I'm touching you now," Vaslav said, the edge in his voice creeping through the phone to kiss her like sharp knives raking lightly over her skin. A threat, of sorts, but it still felt delicious. "And if it matters at all, because I am not above using various manipulations to get my way, I haven't slept in just about as many days. Don't act like you won't enjoy giving me this."

"You'd be mad," she said. "Out of your mind."

"What's your point? *That's nothing new.*"

"And just how is that the *least* I could do?" Vera asked, grinning.

Even if he couldn't see it.

Vaslav growled a frustrated sound. "Vera, I am *still* looking the picture. Of course, red looks the way it does on you, you've got porcelain for skin."

His compliment tugged at her weak self-control. "Where exactly are you while you're looking at it, huh?"

"In my den."

Alone, then.

Shocker.

"You didn't answer me, though," she pointed out. "How is this the very least I could do for you?"

"You're *teasing* me, kitten," Vaslav said, his gravely accent twisting the English equivalent of his pet name for her into something that knotted heavily in her gut. Like the lust settling there, too. "And I promise the next time we sit down together, I'll make you regret it."

"But are you going to answer me?"

His chuckle rumbled on the phone.

Dark.

So deep.

Vera had little doubts about whether or not she'd enjoy how he made her regret this. Talk about making something worth her damned while …

"This is the very least you could do for me," Vaslav replied, every word confident and clipped as she imagined them slipping past his smirking lips, "because I think I've been very patient with you while your friend visits. I've repeatedly considered dragging you out to Dubna just to keep you locked upstairs with me for a few days, because we both know how much you value the concept of time when you're in bed with me, but I was trying not to be selfish. That could change. *Today*, even. I bet I could get the Rolls to the city in less than an hour. How opposed are you to being on top in the backseat?"

"Jesus Christ," Vera swore in a laugh. "Igor takes at least an hour and a half, and he drives like a madman."

"Like one. Except he isn't."

Vera's teeth cut into her upper lip with a pleasing sting. The same way Vaslav liked to bite her on that very spot, too just to take a gasp or hiss from her.

"Just tell me if you're wet," he urged.

Demanded, was more like it.

"I'm honestly trying to ignore it," Vera replied, mindful of her voice level.

She also hadn't lied.

The squirm of her crossed legs made the dampness of the soft lace between her thighs more apparent.

She had yet to take her hand off the armrest, though, and she still needed the one holding the phone. Or that's what she kept telling herself.

Vaslav released relief in an exhale, muttering, "Then, here's what you're going to do for me, sweetest thing, I want the red set sent straight to me. After you get your hand in those panties and rub one, or wait—"

"*Wait for what?*"

She hadn't even bothered to let him finish. If only she cared about the desperation that snuck into her tone.

Vaslav laughed. "Is your hand down there now?"

"*No.*"

Vera couldn't take her eyes off her own reflection in the mirror. Those nerves fluttering in her belly were practically invisible to the woman wrapped in sin sitting across from her. She seemed more womanly than Vera thought herself to be, sexiness smothered her every movement and blink. Except that woman absolutely was her.

"I only said wait because I wanted to ask how fast could you get yourself to three?" he asked.

Vera's tongue smacked the roof of her mouth. "Orgasms?"

"Mmm."

"Three minutes. Maybe four."

He whistled low.

Pleased.

Vera would be a liar if she said that sound didn't aide in the sudden gush of heat between her thighs when she rubbed them together.

"I need at least three, then," he said, "hand—or *hands*—in the panties. They better smell like you,

Vera. Soft like petals and *wet*. Fold the panties under the bra and stockings, tie the bow pretty and neat, and take it to one of those nice women at the front who I know have been helping you all day. They'll be all too happy to take the box with the red set and drive it out to my estate for the price I will pay. Don't worry, they already know that price is whatever they ask. They won't open the box, and neither will Mira when they deliver it to her at the end of the driveway."

Vera rubbed her lips together as the side of her hand stroked back and forth on the armrest of the chair. "Just you?"

"I promise. And we won't talk about what I'll use them for tonight, either. I'll have it all dry-cleaned. Don't worry."

"You're disgusting."

"And you love it," he returned. "Stop pretending like the little slut inside of you isn't *weeping* right now. The only thing you're missing is me there to do it for you. How wet are you?"

Of course, he asked that then. As she slipped her fingers under the waistband of her panties; like he somehow knew when her fingertips glided over her clit and between her slick slit. Had he heard her readjust on the chair when she uncrossed her legs and opened them wide?

"*What do you see?*" Vaslav asked.

"I'm wet all the way through the gusset and lace."

He groaned thickly.

She used two fingers at first, working them in with wet, soppy sounds that she didn't know if he could hear. Her breaths hitched with every roll of her wrist to get her fingers deeper. She should be ashamed of the wet spot she was going to leave on the chair but at least the leather would allow her to easily wipe it away.

"Talk to me," he said, hoarser than ever.

"Three f-fingers, now," she whispered.

"They're not like mine, are they?"

"No."

Not calloused, or long. She found flex and give in her fingers and hand that his did not provide; he took with no forgiveness.

"But you'll still um," he told her, almost soothing.

"*For you.*"

Voice crackling.

Body trembling.

Her back stayed turned to a door she couldn't even remember if she had locked, but it didn't matter to Vera. Not then.

"I *really* shouldn't send these to you," she whimpered. "Besides, Hannah's flying out this weekend. Saturday morning. I could be there with you—"

"Saturday afternoon. You damn well *better.*" Vaslav's husky laugh helped to tether Vera over the very precious ledge keeping her from falling into her first orgasm. "And as for the panties and the rest, well, we both know exactly what you're going to do. Was that one?"

She gasped out a yes, hips still jerking into her trembling, thrusting hand.

"Good girl," her dangerously addictive lover praised, "now stroke your clit for two but first, tell me how you taste."

18.

I hate the snow. I hate the snow. I hate the snow.

Vaslav had always been better suited for warmer weather. His mother took him on a vacation to a private island in the Maldives when he was barely six, and a part of him never left those warm beaches. His mood drastically improved based on the temperature outside. There was absolutely no way to ignore the cold creeping into his bones when the snow started to fall from the wide-open skies.

The one thing he hated more than snow and cold weather was his migraines, but as he'd stopped self-medicating his constant pain, Vaslav was left with his ever-constant companion throughout many of his days. At least, while he rested lounging on the wide steps at the front of the house, the falling snow gave him something else to scowl about.

For the moment.

He could always get back to the migraines later, after all. It wasn't like they would soon leave.

"Look at it," he bitched under his breath. "All *white* and *wet*."

Igor grunted where he worked at the rear of the parked SUV. "And cold."

"And that *and that, too!*"

"*Hmm*."

The inquisitive note from Igor had Vaslav sitting up on the steps. The thickness of his tweed coat was not nearly enough to keep him protected from the quickly plummeting temperatures, but he barely shivered when a good gust of chilly wind sent snowflakes dancing over the steps.

And *him*.

Fuck the cold.

He had other things to focus on now.

"What was that for?" he asked Igor. "That *hmm*."

"Were you playing with the cash?"

Ah.

Vaslav fell back to the snowy steps, even more unpleasant by how much had managed to gather on the stone in the fifteen minutes that he'd been outside. "I may have broken a few bands here and there, tossed around some bills ..."

"A few?" Igor asked, leaning back far enough that Vaslav could see the way he arched an eyebrow in question. "More like damn near every one. In all six bags, Vas. I wondered why the duffels were lumpier."

He didn't see the problem. Checking the stacks upon stacks of bills served a purpose. More than one, even, and he didn't intend on sharing them with Igor.

"Lucky for your accountant that I didn't find anything wrong, no?" Vaslav returned.

Igor sighed, leaning back into the rear hatch of the SUV with a grumbled *bullshit* or something of a similar sort. Louder, he told his boss, "The neuroticism is getting out of hand. If you're willing to talk to the doctor about other things, perhaps that's something else you could bring up, yeah? I'm just saying. You could have picked rolls at random and checked, you didn't have to check every fucking one. There's a hundred million dollars here in various bills. Is this *all* you did for the week?"

Vaslav waved Igor's nonsense off. He didn't need to be reminded that he could have spent his week, and his current Friday night, doing a hundred other things than what he had and currently was. "I was bored, and had nothing else better to do."

For a few too many nights.

He blamed Vera for that.

And her little friend, Hannah, too.

Just because Vaslav accepted the fact that Vera had a life outside of the one he created between him and her didn't mean he liked it. He was not particularly good at sharing things. Especially if said thing happened to be a woman he thought about for nearly every waking second of his days. She probably featured in a great deal of his dreams, too, when he was lucky enough to have them, but if Igor wanted to talk about things getting out of hand with Vaslav, *this* was a far better topic.

"It's not normal," he uttered.

The zip of bags followed Igor stepping back from the SUV and yanking the rear hatch shut. "What isn't?"

"How often I find myself thinking about Vera."

Or maybe it wasn't *healthy*. That was a better word. Normal was a state of mind Vaslav hadn't been able to relate to in decades, so perhaps that wasn't the best point of reference.

"It's all the time," he added when Igor kept quiet, allowing his boss to speak. "About stupid things, too. How she's put her hair today, or what she's wearing. I even wonder if she's eating!"

Which might not be a bad thing if it wasn't constant. The obsessive thoughts only eased when Vera was near enough for him to see and touch, but that was because then he could focus all that energy and silent fixation into reality.

Igor's lifting brow said what he didn't. The sight alone was enough to irritate Vaslav to the ends of the earth and back. He knew how he sounded, he didn't need Igor's fucking expression to spell it out, too.

"Stop looking at me like that," he muttered.

Igor cleared his throat. "I'm not looking at you—"

"You are like *that*. Big eyes and high eyebrows. Just because you don't speak doesn't mean I can't *hear*."

"Hear *what*?"

The sight of a black mass bounding around the corner of the house stopped Vaslav from answering the question. Marrow, with snowflakes clinging to his shaggy black hair, made his way along the side of the house until he came to the steps where he took them one at a time to the very top. Never once did the pup look at Igor, and he certainly didn't bother with Vaslav.

At the front door, Marrow plunked his heavy backside down, tipped his snout high, and started to howl. One long whine after another. Each louder than the last.

Igor cringed at the sound. "Another reason to hate the winter ... that thing likes the house."

"He's not a thing."

"He's not a normal dog, either," Igor returned just as fast. "He'd be shot anywhere else, Vas. No one would put up with him the way you do."

Well …

Maybe the dog was just misunderstood.

On his fifth howl, Marrow turned until his dark eyes found Vaslav. It was almost like the dog's soul was screaming through his black eyes for his master to listen—*get me the fuck out of here*. Vaslav wasn't the only beating heart on the property that hated the snow more than the sight of their own reflection.

"I know, it's hard when the bunnies turn white, and you can't see them in the snow, huh?" he asked the dog.

Marrow howled at that, too.

Vaslav cackled right back.

Finally, the front door opened a crack. Barely an inch, but it stopped Marrow's howl instantly. Suddenly, the usually feral and wild dog was an overgrown puppy, and he laid himself flat to the stone step with a fast-wagging tail. He whined at the woman eyeing him from beyond the front door.

Mira tried to keep a serious face. "Is it cold?"

Marrow didn't move. Except for his tail.

He didn't make a sound, either.

"Shake first," Mira said.

Standing the moment the words left her lips, Marrow turned into a ball of shuddering black fur and tumbling snowflakes. A second later, the door opened wider, and the dog stepped into the darkness inside. All the while, his fluffy tail wagged.

Igor shook his head when Vaslav turned back around with a chuckle.

"He barely even nips at her when he wants

something like being let inside," Igor pointed out. "See, he can be nice when he chooses to be. He never does that for me."

"Jealousy is unbecoming."

That had his man scoffing.

Hard.

"Right," Igor choked out in a laugh. "A fucking joke, that."

The noise between the men settled down while Igor hit the auto start on the SUV, and the engine purred to life. The smoke sputtered from the tailpipe, the only source of heat in the bitter chill of the air.

Igor checked his watch. "I better head out, then. You think?"

Vaslav didn't even care about the time, or the length of it that it would take Igor to arrive at the meeting place. "What's it matter if you're late? The prick isn't about to complain when he thinks you're delivering him a hundred million dollars. Whether it's five minutes or thirty, Feliks Abramov won't give a shit as long as you show up."

The bastard was who he was. Greedy to an extreme. Never willing to turn the chance to get one up on someone else down. If getting what he wanted meant doing exactly what he thought he had to, no excuses even if the demands by Vaslav included a last-minute meeting in practically the middle of nowhere to collect his money owed, then that's precisely what Feliks would do. In the end, the man's behaviors and motives stemmed from the same thing regardless of how it presented itself.

Manipulation.

Like leopards, Abramovs also couldn't change their spots. Vaslav expected nothing less.

"A matter of semantics," Igor responded dully.

"Or is it one of respect," Vaslav returned, "that Feliks, mind you, has never deserved."

Igor pondered that statement.

Vaslav let him.

Besides, he needed the moment to massage away some of the tension and pressure forming behind his eyeballs. He regularly considered carrying around a spork just in case the urge to spoon his eyes out of their sockets ever became too much. At this point, he might follow through.

"No matter why I decide to show up on time," Igor said, bringing Vaslav back to the conversation at hand, "at the end of the day, I would just like to get this over and done with."

"Right. One more thing crossed off your growing list."

Igor grunted at that, spinning on his heels to head around the rear of the vehicle. "You said it, boss, not me."

Igor squinted one eye up at the darkening sky. With the sun setting fast, soon the overcast grey would be a black canvas with no stars. Just silent snowfall for God only knew how many days.

"Any change on the weather report?" he asked.

"Expected to be mild next month."

"Yeah, but that's next month," Vaslav mumbled.

"What's that you said?" Igor asked, popping his head over the top of the SUV before he opened the driver's door. "Did you say you wanted to come?"

No. That wasn't what he said at all. Not even close. But it wasn't a bad idea.

"I suppose I better come," Vaslav said, pushing off the steps to stand and taking the time to brush the wayward snowflakes from his jacket and dark wash denim jeans. It was the only time of year he cared to wear such a heavy, irritating fabric because it did okay in the cold. "Wouldn't want you hitting a bump or something, and ruining everything before Feliks realizes what I've done."

Igor's blank stare over the roof of the SUV didn't waver from Vaslav as he approached the vehicle. It was only once Vaslav came to stand at the passenger door that his head of security glanced to the rear with concern writing lines on his brow and bald head.

"*You* wanted to load the duffels up," Igor said.

Bored with the obvious, Vaslav didn't respond and instead, wrenched open the passenger side door.

"All the bands are cut, and the bags are diff—"

"Are we driving, or no?" Vaslav asked.

Igor openly glowered. "At least tell me what shit we're about to step in before we do it."

Vaslav grinned. "Trust me, this is better to watch."

19.

"Would you have done it?" Igor asked.

Vaslav passed the plaque at his side a disinterested glance. Gold lettering in Russian and English spelled out the historic nature of the site, and the still present dangers because no one had the funds or means to tear it down. The government sure as hell didn't care.

Igor leaned closer to inspect the small memorial.

"What, jumped off the bridge?" Vaslav asked.

Igor shrugged, murmuring the names under his breath of kids who had drowned after jumping—whether the current took them, they had been tangled in something under the water, or they jumped into something just beneath the surface; they each got a spot for their name.

And an unfortunate series of dates. One year after another. Nearly all the months looked the same. *Summer.* Strangely, it was also not a spot that saw a lot of suicides.

"Yeah, would you?" Igor asked. "I could see you

doing it, had you been given the chance."

"Almost, one summer."

Igor stood up straight at that. "Really?"

The old, forgotten covered wooden bridge, or the half left still standing on worn and broken cement blocks, just outside of Dubna's town limits was a menace to the teenagers of every generation, and the parents who buried them year after year. A risk any rebel couldn't pass up. To jump from a hundred feet into what seemed like bottomless black waters had become a rite of passage for only the boys and girls who had the most reckless and wild hearts.

Yet, for every ten that dared to take the plunge, it was said that an average of two wouldn't come back up. Only to be found later caught up in a dam upstream.

Despite knowing that what remained of the fallen half of the bridge was still under the calm waters of the stretch of Volga River, ignorant youth, and undoubtedly stupid pride drove kids to walk the fifty rickety feet to make the jump. A sad state of affairs and too much danger prevented the people of the area from taking matters into their own hands and pulling down the bridge. It was a shame, because back before the kids used the rickety edge to jump off, the water down below had been a popular swimming hole.

Even standing at the mouth's edge of the old bridge, with its large entrance eave beams blackened with age overhead, Vaslav couldn't honestly say he would have made the jump in his own youth.

"A guy drowned the day before, but since he didn't show up at the dam, they had a few boats in the water." Vaslav shrugged, adding, "I don't think I could have done it if I was standing there, though; they put me in the colony before the next summer, so I never had to find out."

Igor's grin faded, and he swiped his palm down his mouth and jaw as he eyed the quiet, short road leading to the remnants of the bridge that connected off from the main trek. While the neighboring townships had erected barricades to block the road, they didn't do much good. Someone could easily fit a vehicle in between the two cement blocks painted bright yellow.

Vaslav and Igor, on the other hand, had left their SUV running just beyond the safety of the dividers. It left more than enough room for the man of the evening to arrive and follow Vaslav's very specific instructions about how he should pull up to receive his payment.

"Looks like we didn't have to worry about time at all," Vaslav said as Igor rolled his eyes and stuffed his hands into his parka's pockets. "You're never one to be late, Igor."

"Yeah, well—"

Vaslav's comment had come right on time; the roll of wheels on gravel drew the gazes of both men to the black Porsche pulling off the main road. The headlamps on the car flicked off as the driver navigated the vehicle in a half turn so he could back up beyond the cement dividers keeping the bridge blocked.

Feliks' Porsche came to a stop only a foot from Vaslav and Igor's feet. The trunk of the car popped open a second before the driver's door opened wide and out stepped a man Vaslav would forever call a coward.

"Feliks," Igor greeted.

The only living Abramov took his time closing the driver's door and joining the two men waiting at the rear of the car. Despite directing his words to Vaslav, his gaze didn't leave the six duffels sitting just inside the mouth of the bridge on the ground.

"I didn't know you were also making a trip out to see me tonight," Feliks said. "Am I that special, Vaslav?"

"Or that unlucky," he returned frankly.

Feliks, quick like he was, took the subtle threat for what it could be. He put his hands up, averting his eyes from Vaslav's unforgiving stare when he said, "No harm meant, of course."

Vaslav didn't bother with a reply.

Igor stepped up to the plate, still ready to get on with the evening and remove one more thing from his unofficial to-do list. "Took six bags. All various bills. Should make distributing it easier, however you choose."

Feliks nodded, his gaze back on the duffels. Right where Vaslav expected it to be. "I have plans for it. It'll go far with renovations, and funding at the school. Although, the kids will be sad that Vera isn't returning."

Every word the man let slip out of his mouth was a lie. Vaslav knew it, too.

Vaslav spoke up, then. "Don't worry Vera's got her hands full of other things to do."

For now, he added silently.

Feliks, stuffing his hands into his slacks pockets, eyed the darkness beyond the mouth of the bridge. "Rumor is, part of what's keeping her hands full is *you*. Someone might even be getting married soon.

She's kind-hearted, and entirely too good for you."

A laugh split from Vaslav's lips. "You're not wrong. Let me guess how word traveled, my mother?"

"She's making calls to anyone who will take them. I just happened to put two and two together about who the wife-to-be in question actually was," Feliks returned.

Fucking bitch.

"Her circle isn't that large," Igor assured.

It didn't even matter.

Not at this point.

"They're not so heavy if you give 'em a good throw," Vaslav said to Feliks as he passed the man by, referring to the duffels he left behind. Igor was quick to follow Vaslav. "Maybe pull the Porsche back a few more inches."

Feliks didn't move as Vaslav and Igor headed for their own vehicle, parked and running, twenty or so feet away. Pulling himself into the passenger seat, he watched the man near the bridge reach for the first blue duffel bag at the same time Igor climbed into the driver's side of the SUV.

"He was going to run with it," Vaslav told Igor when the man slammed the door shut. "The money, I mean."

Igor glanced his way, but his stare skipped past to the window and the scene beyond. "How in the hell do you know that? I've been watching Feliks, I keep tabs on him like anybody else that might be a problem."

"He lied about what he was going to do with the money. Didn't you tell me last week that there hasn't even been a contractor visit The Swan House to survey and estimate the damage from the last water leak? That was months ago, Igor."

"That doesn't explain how you know—"

"I still have both deeds to his Swan House," Vaslav interjected. "More importantly, I have the original, which should matter to him the most, no?"

Igor fell further into the seat with a grunt. "Right, because he doesn't know about the fake."

"I found it behind a lock in a cabinet that was *very* easy to break. He had to have noticed it was gone by now, but he didn't say a thing. He's willing to pretend like it doesn't even matter as long as he gets the thing that he wants."

The money.

Just like all those years ago with Irina. Some shit never changed. Feliks had been all too willing to ignore the signs of danger facing his own sister as long as the money on the table was a substantial enough number to make him turn his cheek.

All it would have taken him was a single phone call; a second out of his day to tell Irina not to leave the house that day. She never even saw it coming.

So, neither did Feliks.

Vaslav left the useless excuse of life alive long enough for the man to think he was safe, estranged from his old world, sure, and a pariah to everyone else, but safe from Vaslav's remaining wrath nonetheless.

No one was safe.

"Too bad for him," Vaslav said, turning to watch as Feliks tossed the first heavy bag of bills into the trunk of his car. "He won't even get the money out of me."

That had been decided the moment Vaslav made the offer to Feliks, money for his disconnection from

Vera Avdonin, and the bastard hadn't even known it. The first bag being tossed into the back of the Porsche was all it took to start a chain reaction.

One of the most interesting things Vaslav learned in the juvenile colony was how mixing specific compounds could produce various results. One sealed glass beaker inside another filled with reactive, dangerous chemicals could easily create a plume of fire when thrown hard enough to break.

The first fireball that came rushing out of the trunk sent Feliks flying back, arms flailing, into the waiting bags right behind him. Small fire-like explosions started one after another as each mini-bomb inside the bags were broken, and the chemicals mixed.

"Well, get going," Vaslav said when the fire caught onto the bridge, *and* the back of Feliks' running Porsche. It was a fire that only needed the chemical to splatter, spreading the caustic liquid and licking flames further to continue burning.

The bridge.

The Porsche.

The ground.

Feliks.

He didn't care about the man screaming and jerking back and forth on the ground.

Igor pulled the SUV out of park, and hit the gas as the first backfire from the exhaust of Feliks' overheating Porsche cracked through the air. The car exploded before they had the chance to pull out on the road. In the passenger door mirror, the sky lit up from the fire and the sight of cash fluttering into the air made Vaslav chuckle.

What went up had to come down. The river would catch the fluttering, burning money—or what was left by the end of it all and take it straight to the canal.

"I'd rather this entire country wipe their asses with my money than give it to that man," Vaslav said. Well, now they had something in the range of a hundred million to do so. "Let them bitch about bodies in the canal *now*."

"We really need to get a handle on how you deal with your problems," Igor muttered as they drove further from the scene. "I'm not going to believe you when you tell me you're dealing with something. You're absolutely *not* dealing with it, Vas."

Vaslav disagreed. This had gone better than he expected. "Can't imagine *why*."

Not to mention …

"You had every chance to stop me on the way here," Vaslav said.

The man in the driver's seat didn't deny the truth.

Slowly, whether Igor realized it or not, his boss gave him more and more rope to work with. How he used that rope was up to him, of course. Igor could hang himself with it, or the rest of the world. That didn't change what remained proverbially tied to the end of the rope, however.

The keys.

To a kingdom.

"I want to retire," Vaslav said, lost in the passing darkness blanketed in a layer of new, fresh snow. "It's not like the brotherhood would miss me. Haven't I earned a few quiet, happy years of my own making?"

Coated in desperation, Igor laughed. "Is that what all of this is about … *really*?"

What else mattered?

20.

The airport bustled with activity, but Vera only studied the reflection of Hannah's frowning face in the glass overlooking a snowy car park. Sitting side by side on bench seats in front of the windows, the two friends were far enough away from the rest of the people milling about that no one even glanced their way.

"You should have gone through security fifteen minutes ago," Vera pointed out.

Hannah scrunched up her nose at the idea. "I've still got time."

"Right, when you're supposed to be at your gate an hour before."

"We both know they call passengers for at least another half hour. I can get to my gate in time from here. Don't worry."

"Or are you just not ready to leave?" Vera asked.

Might as well get straight to the point. Hannah never minded her friend's bluntness before. This time wasn't the exception.

"I didn't think I'd miss Moscow this much," Hannah admitted. "This city was the first place I really … I don't know, *grew up*. I learned how to make it my home, and nobody ever made me think I didn't belong."

"I know that feeling."

All too well.

"But then with Viktor, he made sure nothing about Moscow felt like my home," Hannah added quieter.

Vera didn't want Hannah to go back down that painful road. "What's your mom doing about the extra security she's had on you?"

"I don't really need it, so. I'll be glad to see them go."

Hannah shrugged under her many thick layers; she refused to wear a parka or another suitable coat for the weather. Instead, she opted for a thick wool shawl covering her equally warm hoodie. She added a matching hat, scarf and mittens to the set, but Vera couldn't say she'd brave the weather wearing the same. Even if Hannah assured she was more than comfortable under all the layers. Whatever floated her friend's boat.

"I might move back," Hannah whispered.

The promise was like a warm hug around Vera's broken heart. Life had not been the same since Hannah raced out of the country practically overnight. She missed her best friend, and while Vera hadn't really lost Hannah, so to speak, phone calls were not the same as having her near. Virtual could never replace reality.

"Would you?" Vera pressed.

Hannah nodded. "To be honest, I need time away

from my mom, too. It's not like she's a whole lot better than my ex-husband, but at least she never beat the shit out of me the way he did. Nothing's ever good enough for her."

"Toxicity still kills."

Just in a different way.

Vera cringed at the sight of a car's rear end skidding back and forth on an icy patch in the car park. Hannah, on the other hand, laughed when she noticed the driver's predicament, saying, "He needs chains on those tires."

Glancing her friend's way, Vera said, "You know, if you don't want to worry about having a place to stay, and wouldn't mind the occasional roommate" — Hannah turned away from the window, then, meeting Vera's gaze— "then my villa is open. I'm moving to Dubna after Vas and I get married. The villa's fine to sit for a while, but a home needs a heartbeat to really live."

Or that's what her mother always said. Claire even kept the family's many properties around the world rented throughout the year with cleaning staff that went in regularly between tenants when the homes were empty.

"Dubna isn't *too* far," Hannah muttered. "I suppose."

"In a way, I feel like I've only just met him, but he's exactly where I want to be. So, I guess now I just want to spend the rest of my time with Vaslav learning all the stuff I skipped over before I fell in love with him."

"God, I can't see you moving *all* those plants, either."

"You've not seen how big the house in Dubna is,

but I think I've got a few rooms to fill. The ones at the villa can stay. As long as you learn when to water them. I know there's a lot, but it's really not that hard."

Except the lilac shrub. She would bring Irina home for Vas. They could find a new spot for the bench and bush.

Hannah laughed; it was lighter the second time. "You won't hate me if I kill a few in the process? Because I might, it's a real possibility."

"Is that a yes?" Vera returned with a grin.

Her friend's face, full of freckles while her emerald eyes twinkled, lit up with her laughter all over again. "Yeah, why not? I'll move in and water your damn plants."

Then, Hannah's laughter fell short as she eyed Vera. "But you're the occasional roommate, right?"

"I'm the roommate."

She opted not to mention that Kiril might still be up in the air on that side of things. Who knew what the next weeks and months would bring?

"And you *will* be back for the wedding, right?" Vera asked.

Hannah had the audacity to roll her eyes. "I picked a dress and everything, didn't I?"

*

"What's all that about?" Vera asked.

The train of transport vehicles hauling heavy equipment, flagged on both ends by police presence, caught Vera's attention as it passed their vehicle on the road leading into Dubna going the opposite way.

Kiril didn't even glance sideways, keeping his eyes

firmly on the road ahead of them as he steered the SUV over icy roads. "Who the hell would know? I heard an old bridge got burned down last night, something about a car catching fire, or whatever."

"What?"

The teen only shrugged.

Vera tried not to think about it despite watching the line of eighteen-wheelers shrink in the passenger mirror. "I hope nobody got hurt."

"Didn't hear anything about a body."

"No?"

Kiril shook his head. "Nope. Just a *lot* of fucking money."

Huh.

"How much money?" Vera asked, honestly curious.

"All I know is that when I got a call from a buddy in town warning me about the blockade on the road to Dubna this morning, I was told not to ask questions. Because nobody was offering any answers."

"Where was the money? In the car?"

Again, the kid shook his head.

"Nah," he said, lifting one hand from the steering wheel to point his index finger downward. "They found it down in the water."

Vera didn't have anything to say to that because nothing Kiril said made a whole lot of sense. Besides, in less than twenty minutes, she'd be exactly where she wanted to be again, with Vas. And what did a burned bridge or car, and mysterious money in the river, have anything to do with that?

Very little, likely.

She hoped.

*

Vera did not expect to find Vaslav waiting on the front steps when Kiril parked the SUV at the bottom. It was the soft smile that tugged at the better side, better meaning it showed more emotion than its scarred counterpart, of Vaslav's lips that had her heart picking up the pace of its beats at the very sight of him.

She barely had time to admire the way the Pashkov property looked cloaked in a blanket of white snow before Vaslav distracted her.

Kiril, already stepping out of the vehicle to grab the one bag Vera had packed while Hannah was readying her luggage the night before, didn't seem offended that she left him to do a job she was more than capable of handling herself.

Vaslav met Vera on the middle steps.

One higher than hers.

She had to look up at him even more from where she stood, and Vaslav didn't appear to mind the extra height it afforded him what with the way he winked down at her.

"Hannah's flown out, has she?" Vaslav asked, his blue gaze sweeping over her face.

"Oh, she's not *the friend* now?"

"Do you want her to be?"

His easy banter, and lack of a scowl, made her believe he wasn't suffering too much. She could always tell when one of his eyes squinted, but both were wide open. And locked on her.

"I want a kiss," she replied. "That's what I'd really like."

He reached for her at the same time he replied,

236

"Done deal."

Vaslav caught the underside of Vera's jaw in his large hands, keeping her head tilted up for him as he bent down to press three kisses, one after another, against her grinning mouth. When he leaned in for the fourth, she parted her lips and teased him with her tongue.

He kissed the tip of that, too.

"Mira's made a late lunch," he told her, still not pulling away. Instead, he dotted soft kisses along her forehead, each one melting her into a puddle of sappy happiness, murmuring, "I'll meet you inside, hmm? Get out of the cold."

She didn't even feel it.

Not with him.

A muffled *thunk* finally yanked Vera away from Vaslav. She turned on the steps to see Kiril had dropped her bag at the bottom.

The teen looked at Vaslav, waiting. "Igor said you had a job or something for me?"

"Right," her lover muttered.

Vaslav stepped beyond Vera on the stone stairs, pinched her chin on his way by, and dragged her in for another quick kiss. After he let her go, he gestured at the front door. The maroon paint stood out far more in the chill of surrounding snow. "Don't wait for me to eat, yeah?"

Vera nodded. "Okay."

She climbed the remaining steps to the top as Vaslav headed down. At the front door, she pushed it open, and glanced back just in time to see Vaslav pick up her bag from the ground. With his other hand, he reached for an inner pocket on his blazer. The wad of cash he handed over, a significantly sized roll of bills, only partially hid the other item he produced. A tri-folded paper.

Neither man at the bottom of the steps noticed that she had yet to enter the house, but Vera knew better than to linger. Just because she was curious didn't mean she needed all the answers. Sometimes, that did more harm than good.

Vera started to close the door as Kiril flicked the paper open, and Vaslav produced a similarly sized envelope from his inner pocket as well. She didn't miss the widening of Kiril's eyes when he scanned whatever he found on the paper, and muttered, "Oh, *shit.*"

"I'm sure you can get that, and these documents as well, back to the office where they belong, yes?" Vaslav asked. "There's only one of those in the city, after all. What more do you need me to say?"

"Not a thing, boss."

"And if you get asked, what the fuck do you know about it, yeah?"

"Not one damn thing," Kiril replied just as fast.

"Make sure of it."

She didn't wait to hear more.

The door clicked shut first.

*

"Should the fact you can multitask when your ass is stuffed full with my fingers hurt my ego?" Vaslav asked.

Vera muffled her giggle into the side of her hand as she finished scribbling her last thought onto her notebook, a list of tasks for next week that she didn't want to forget. "You were the one who said you wanted to try something. I was just over here trying to sleep."

With her chin still resting in her palm, Vera turned to laugh at Vaslav when he tipped his head toward the pillow beside his. "You mean, over there, yeah? And don't lie, there was a reason you brought your notebook and pen with you."

"Shut up."

Her playful quip earned her a sudden third finger between the tight ring of muscles he had been working to loosen for nearly ten minutes, and a stinging slap on her right ass cheek that had Vera sucking in a lungful of hissed air.

Vaslav squeezed the still burning cheek until Vera peeked back at him, and only then did he loosen his grip. "*Be nice.*"

"Well, how long are you going to do that before you just *fuck* me?"

She was looking forward to it.

He liked her boldness if his husky laugh was any indication. His fingers stopped pumping into her backside, and his thumb and pinky fingers cupped her rear; slick and oily from the new jar of coconut oil that he'd produced from a bedside drawer earlier.

Apparently, Mira had already been informed not to go looking for that one.

With his legs crossed, and hers spread wide around him on the bed sheets, all it took was his hand sliding up her shivering spine for him to lock her in place as he bent down for a kiss. He dropped two. One on each dimple at her lower back.

His words murmured against her skin. "Maybe I was letting you finish your little list, *kisska.*"

"For the record, *this* kitten isn't going anywhere

near your dick after you stick it in my ass. Not before you clean it."

That earned her another swat.

Vera just laughed back.

"Fair enough," Vaslav still conceded.

His fingers started working into her ass again reminding Vera how sensitive her body became when all he did was touch her. Especially intimately. She pushed the notebook away with the tip of the pen, and tossed it further away on the bed after.

"I have things I can't forget to do next week," she breathed, trying to focus more on the words than the way his fingers found something good to hit and tease with every stroke. "Even if I'd like to pretend like I have nothing to do, that's not how it works."

"What do you have to do?"

"A doctor appointment I put off, getting rentals set up for my parents, and—"

"I wouldn't worry about rentals. I think Demyan has it all figured out now."

Vera stilled on the bed, asking, "You talked to my father?"

With his next question, the pumps, his three fingers stretching her rear full, came harder and deeper. "If I say yes, are you going to tell me to stop?"

In most cases, yes, she absolutely would. Vera didn't enjoy bringing the topic of any man, let alone her father, into bed with another. *Wasn't that just good practice?*

"I really wish you'd just get on with fucking me," she whined.

"You're not ready. It'll hurt."

"Have you seen the size of you? It will *always* hurt."

That had him chuckling.

"The doctor's appointment, now what's that for?" he asked, withdrawing his fingers from her ass to resituate his position on the bed. "Here, come up."

Sitting on his shins, he grabbed her waist and tugged to urge Vera to her knees, shuffling her back until his hair-dusted chest kissed her spine, and she could feel his hand pumping his cock below her.

"A checkup, and my usual injection," she said. "Unless you've changed your mind about babies."

"Absolutely not."

Vera cackled out a laugh that died in a moan when he pressed the head of his cock against her ass. That tight ring of muscles had been worked and stretched just enough to let the tip of his shaft slip in an inch or two, but she still felt every one, even if the coconut oil he'd loaded up on had also helped.

Trembling.

And *shivering.*

Of course, it would hurt.

She still liked it.

"I needed advice," she heard him say behind her, his words chopping and breathless in her ear. "And that's why I called your father. It felt like an appropriate source to start with, considering."

Considering what?

Why would he want to go back to that conversation now? Didn't she have better things to think about when his hands grabbed fistfuls of her ass, and that was the only thing keeping her steady?

"Easy," he told her, his voice a soothing balm to the pain that licked up her spine. He wasn't all that deep inside of her, but it sure felt like it. He pointed to the image of the two reflected back in the decorative wall mirror across from the bed. "Watch me make you take this nice and slow, my love."

Legs shaking, she worked a little more of his cock inside of her as she seated further down his shaft. It felt the same way it had earlier. *Too much*. The sharpest, hottest sting. Yet, she wanted it.

"Am I?" Vera's lips grazed over Vaslav's scarred cheek when he leaned forward over her shoulder. "Am I your love?"

"Whatever's left of it, anyway. Every bit of it is yours."

His arms wrapped tight around her, holding her close and helping take the pressure and weight off her weak legs while he nuzzled his face in her neck. Before long, he had her rocking on him, taking more of him deeper every time she fell back onto his cock.

Despite the licks of pain, and with his hand falling between her thighs so his fingers would work fast circles over her clit, she could already taste the bittersweet bliss.

"W-why would you call my f-father for advice?" Vera asked between hitched breaths and the slap of skin on slick, hot skin. By the time he had seated himself deep enough that her insides ached, he gave her little to no time to adjust. At that point, she really didn't care if she even needed it. Anything to have him fucking her.

Vaslav laughed darkly, lapping at her neck and gifting her earlobe with the nip of his teeth. "I knew you didn't forget, smart girl."

"*Vas*. Just tell me."

"From one *vor* to another, how exactly do men like us retire?"

His fingers worked her faster, the pressure change giving her exactly what she needed to orgasm in the seconds following. Taking with it what breath she had left.

Probably on purpose.

She didn't think he wanted an answer. Not from her.

21.

The last time Vera woke up to the sound of men's murmurings, she'd wished more than anything that she had simply gone back to sleep. That was her first thought when she sleepily eyed the stairwell leading down from the master suites into the rear of Vaslav's dark den.

Yet, she didn't turn around.

Vera stepped into the stairwell, her fingers ghosting along the smooth railing that had been attached to the wood paneled wall on her way down. Maybe it was the familiar voices both, not just Vaslav that she recognized, and didn't think the conversation was something she shouldn't hear. It wasn't usual for Igor to join Vas in his den for something or other.

Just not so late.

What time is it?

Vera hadn't really checked the clock on the bedside table before slipping out of bed and padding into the bathroom. On her way to the bathroom, she'd first heard the murmurings coming from downstairs. She could count on one hand the number of times she woke up in Valsav's bed without him beside her. Even if he woke up sick, *she* was there.

She quickly realized, once she was halfway down the stairs, why she could hear the murmurings in the suites upstairs. The two men talked so loudly, yelled, really, that they couldn't even be trying to keep it private.

In her opinion, anyhow.

"You know how this goes, he talks, it's *over*."

"Vas—"

"If he fucking talks, Igor, it is *over*. There's nothing to discuss about it. There's nothing else to say."

"There's far more to say and you know it!" the man shouted back at Vaslav.

Vera had no intentions of eavesdropping. She learned her lesson the first time with Vaslav and his Italian business partner. As she came to stand in the small alcove leading from the rear hallway into the den, she didn't hide her presence. Clearing her throat, she leaned against the trim of the wall's corner, and folded her arms over her chest.

"It's late," Vera said.

One man sat behind the large desk, *Vas*. The other, Igor, stood just beyond the large carpet where Vaslav's desk was positioned in the middle. Neither seemed all that interested in her, but that didn't bother Vera.

"And you're yelling," she added after a moment.

She didn't point out that both had been doing the shouting.

Did she need to?

Vaslav, with his fingers clasped together in front of

his face, elbows resting on the desk, was careful not to meet Igor's gaze before turning to glance at Vera. "Go back to bed, *kisska*."

"Are you coming, too?"

He didn't reply.

Vera arched an eyebrow, but Vaslav's stare dropped from hers. Even the man across from the front of the desk wouldn't meet her eyes at that moment.

What had she missed?

"What time is it?" she asked.

"A little after three," Igor replied.

"In the morning?"

"*Da.*"

The darkness outside the windows of the den proved Igor's statement to be true, but that didn't mean Vera was able to process the late time or the reasons for the two men's current argument, either.

"What's happening?" Vera asked. "Something happened, right?"

Neither man spoke.

They didn't even move a muscle.

Their lack of communication didn't exactly sit right with Vera, considering it left her with a heaviness in her stomach that had little to nothing to do with the throbbing ache she still felt in her backside.

Why else would Igor be at Vaslav's home at three in the goddamn morning? The man made the trip from the city to Dubna almost daily, usually every morning and evening, but she couldn't remember a time when he showed up at an ungodly hour like this.

Or hell …

Maybe he did, but it never woke her up before.

"Could you at least tell me if something is wrong?"

she asked.

Vaslav continued staring across his desk at Igor, blankly. "Nothing is wrong. Go to bed, I said."

"Why don't you tell her, Vas?"

Igor's question only served to make Vaslav glower at the man.

"Go on," Igor urged, almost *tauntingly*, "tell her what's happening. What would it hurt?"

"Shut up," Vaslav deadpanned.

It was strange how he could talk without anger or any other emotional inflection, and yet, still make it sound like a threat. Vera, even standing several feet away, shifted uncomfortably on her feet at the heated staring contest between the two men.

"Why won't you tell her what you did?" Igor asked, the only man in the room who seemed willing to let his emotions bleed into his words and tone. Even his stance, tense and ready to spring across the desk, if pushed, vibrated with his anger. "It's not like you're ashamed of it, it was for *her!*"

"What was?" Vera asked, looking at Vas.

Behind the desk, Vaslav's jaw grinded loud enough for her to hear. He didn't look away from Igor, though.

"You're pushing your luck, comrade," Vaslav told the other man. "I indulged your late-night phone call about a problem you know I can't fix at this point, then I was kind enough to invite you into my house at an unacceptable hour just to appease your guilty conscience, and now you want to make demands?"

Igor laughed bitterly. "He's just a kid, Vas. Come on."

"What difference does that make?"

"It makes every difference to me! *Kiril is just a*

fucking kid!"

"I can't help that you feel responsible for the boy," Vaslav responded dully. "I didn't tell you to get him personally involved in your affairs, or mine, for that matter. Those were things you did, and you can't blame me for putting him to good use while I had the chance."

"Is that really what you want to call it?" Igor asked, his tone pitched high.

Vaslav dragged in a lungful of air, and turned to Vera once more. "Please, go up to bed. I'll be there shortly to join you."

Not yet.

Things were just getting interesting.

Or ... *informative.*

"What happened to Kiril? Didn't he have to run something to the city for you?" she asked Vaslav.

His shoulders tensed at the question.

Igor barked a laugh. "Oh, he sure did. Nobody needs a fucking locksmith with that kid on hand, he can pick any lock put in front of his face, right, Vas?"

"Go to bed," Vaslav repeated to Vera, ignoring Igor.

She still didn't move. "Can't you just—"

"*Vera.* That is enough."

Unlike her, Igor wasn't quieted by Vaslav's sharp words.

"He broke into an office in the city to replace some papers that Vaslav had previously taken for reasons he is not willing to divulge, except because *someone* was too impatient to wait, and didn't give him a proper heads up about an important incident from the night before, he wasn't careful," Igor hissed while his pointed stare locked on Vaslav explained exactly who he meant by *someone.*

"I don't understand," Vera admitted.

What did missing papers and someone breaking into an office have anything to do with her?

"Tell her," Igor said, tipping his chin up subtly to appear like he was looking down on Vaslav, "or I will."

"It won't change anything, Igor."

The bald man clenched his teeth, but it wasn't enough to hide the emotion causing his jaw and chin to vibrate with tremors.

"It won't change a thing," Vaslav repeated, shrugging his broad shoulders under the simple grey t-shirt he had pulled on for bed. "Telling her isn't going to make me pick up the phone, and make a call for him because I can't. Kiril knows how this works; if he gets caught, he does the time. Like anybody else in this life."

Vera rubbed away what sleepiness remained in her tired face with the pads of her fingers, all the while, desperately trying to piece together yet another one of Vaslav's many puzzles. Even if he wasn't talking directly to her, he gave away tidbits of information that she couldn't ignore because clearly, every little bit was important.

"You're blatantly disregarding—"

"*What?*" Vaslav interjected heatedly, standing from his desk with two fists slamming down to the top. "What am I disregarding, Igor? That you've toted the fucking kid around like a puppy for the last several months? Or how about that he's had a very intimate and lengthy look at my personal and private life because of it? The very second he was arrested inside that fucking building—"

Squaring his shoulder and jaws, Vaslav calmed his delivery only slightly for what he told Igor next. "He could talk to the *musor—pigs* about anything and everything, and you wouldn't even know it because it was too late the instant he was arrested. He had a choice to make, and you don't know which one it was," Vaslav said, gesturing his arms wide as if he was trying to make Igor understand it was out of his hands. "He's been seen with you just enough to make him a target to anyone that has a problem with you, or me. There is nothing I can do. If he talks, he's dead, and that's the only thing *you* can offer him now. It has practically nothing to do with me. Otherwise, no *vory*, unless he wants it to be known he had dealings with police, is going to touch Kiril until he's out of lock-up."

"Kiril was arrested?"

Neither man acknowledged Vera's question. Separated by only a desk, Vaslav and Igor were too busy staring one another down with heaving chests and clenched fists to pay any attention to her.

Or so she thought.

"*Please,*" Vaslav said, although he didn't turn to her with the request, "go to bed, *kisska.*"

"They caught him leaving the private office of Feliks Abramov at The Swan House," Igor said, his gaze cutting to Vera in the dimly lit den. "While I can guess what he was there to return, Vaslav wouldn't admit it, because that would mean accepting some responsibility for the fact that the cops might very well connect Kiril to an incident he had nothing to do with, and all it would take is a phone call and a *bribe* to get him out of it."

Vera's brow furrowed. "I don't know what you're

talking about."

"Guilty by association is enough to convict Kiril," Igor muttered, although that didn't help with Vera's understanding. "They know who he works for—it's not really a choice, like Vaslav says. If he doesn't talk, *they* put on the pressure. If he does, he'll have to die." Igor glanced at Vaslav again, the anger gone from his pleading expression. "He's seventeen, Vas. He's barely fucking seventeen, and you're expecting a lot out of a boy who isn't even yet a *man*."

"You're looking at the wrong man for pity."

"How about empathy?"

Vaslav scoffed. "Really, what's that?"

"Vas," Vera said, "don't be purposefully mean."

He didn't even glance sideways at her.

"Igor," Vaslav said, "it might only take a call, and more money paid than he's worth to me, but there isn't a soul in Russia today that would do the same for me. They didn't when it *was* me. Don't talk to me about empathy. He made the choice; the expectation is always clear. Unless you're willing for it to be *your* neck and respect on the line for the kid, do not come and ask the same from me. At most, they'll get him on the break and enter with minor theft, if they came up on him with anything. God, it'll barely be a handful of months."

"You don't know that," Igor replied swiftly.

"Why was Kiril at Feliks' office at——"

"Vera, go to fucking bed," Vaslav snapped at her.

Her gaze narrowed right back. "No."

"Why he was there barely even matters," Igor muttered, defeat and sadness coating his every action as he waved and turned around like he was meaning to leave. "What does is that Feliks will never be going back to his office, or that fucking place, and the *musor* already practically know it. If you had just told him when he was here to be careful, that investigators had already been at the bridge in Dubna and identified Feliks' car—"

"The one that burned?" Vera asked.

"*Go to bed!*"

The roar shook the room and rattled her bones.

At that point, Vera didn't really have a choice but to swallow the reply that soured on the back of her tongue with her own bitter anger. Igor exited the den from the main doors, and Vaslav instantly fell back into his seat.

Vaslav didn't tell her to leave again, but too many questions remained for Vera to move. One screamed louder than the rest.

"What if," Vera started to say.

Vaslav lifted his head a fraction of an inch. "What if, *what?*"

"What if Kiril was me?" she asked quietly.

"In custody?"

"Whatever," she replied. "What if it was me?"

"It's not even the same." Vaslav sighed, and scrubbed a hand over his mouth and jaw, mumbling, "It's not the same because I love you. Cement and bars; heaven or hell—nothing will change that, *kisska.*"

What did that change?

Nothing.

"You don't have to love Kiril to care, Vas."

"Who said I didn't care? Vera, it rarely ever comes down to *that.*"

"So, what does?" she asked, not tempering the sarcasm she was sure he'd take as disrespect. "What does it come down to for you to justify a kid getting locked up and taking fault for you, according to Igor, and doing nothing about it?"

Vaslav stood up from the chair, then, his hands flattening to the desk and drawing her gaze in. He'd taken off all his gold rings, leaving his tattooed fingers bare and the upturned spider visible where it took up a good size of space on the back of his hand and wrist. He'd not even bothered to change out of the sweatpants he went to bed in before coming down to see Igor.

"I didn't make Kiril choose this life," Vaslav said, "and I don't determine the price he has to pay for it, either. What that means, no matter the man *or* his age, is the same; a thief is a thief, and if he talks, he's dead. I won't incentivize his silence or release. Not even fear can teach true loyalty. And if I made a call, paid a goddamn bribe, what good would it even do?"

"I would think, to get him *out*, Vas."

Vaslav's knuckles slammed into the desk with a sickening crack that made Vera flinch. "So, single the young thief out. Make him look *special*. Shit, maybe I even give him his stars, and make him untouchable. *What* does that do? Because if he's protected once, the rest of the brotherhood will never let him forget it."

He offered Vera nothing else, and the rough brush of his body against hers as he passed her by ended the conversation altogether for them both.

She didn't follow behind, expecting the crash of Vaslav's emotions to echo overhead as he entered the upstairs suites. Instead, she was greeted by the stomp of his footsteps coming right back down, but far faster than he had initially gone up.

He met her in the stairwell corridor, pinning her against the wall with his expansive, muscled chest and a hand that ghosted over her jaw. The touch wasn't forceful, but his silent demand for her to look up was clear.

Vaslav tilted his head back a bit when their eyes met. "Let me explain, it's the only time I will, why I can't and won't do anything for Kiril "

Vera whispered, "Please do."

She didn't expect him to be frank, detailed, or even truly honest. From the moment she walked into his life, Vaslav had made his affliction to lie or hide things abundantly clear. If it served him, he didn't even blink about it.

Why would this be different?

She forgot, in that moment, that he'd already told exactly why; he loved her.

"Feliks Abramov died by burning to death in the entrance of a bridge that later collapsed. More importantly, he was in possession of a hundred million American dollars that will be traced back to various worldwide bank accounts in the name of Vera Giana Avdonin Pashkov. In three to six months," he said, never once dropping her wildly darting stare, "when Feliks is officially pronounced dead, because they'll never drag him up from where he is, and his estate is handled, paperwork and legal filings will be discovered. Recent documentation that proves the sale and transaction of a certain church, or would you like me to call it your ... little school?"

Her next inhale stung. "That's why Kiril was in Feliks' office? You're not saying ..."

"What exactly does a man gift to the woman who reminds him of heaven?"

Vera's chin trembled in her attempt to hold back the warring emotions threatening to drag her under a current she would not be able to swim. Oh, she wanted to be mad; he deserved that and more. "I never asked you for that."

Vaslav only shrugged. "You didn't have to. Think of it like an early wedding present, no? Welcome to forever."

His palm slid around her neck, and he dropped a bruising kiss against her lips, and helpless to the man she'd allowed to take her heart, she let him. He crushed her to him, even when she didn't kiss him back, but her body melted into his.

As much as a part of her wanted to pull away, she didn't.

"If Kiril doesn't talk," Vera breathed out.

Her lips quivered. She tried so hard to stop.

She couldn't finish the sentence, either. Inside her mind, what she left unspoken still screamed: *I never asked for that.*

"The Swan House," Vaslav replied, kissing her between each word, "is all yours."

22.

Dubna's *"Beauty"* Chapel welcomed guests, and a steady stream of tourists in the warmer months, with wide grey stone and mortar steps that stretched halfway across the front of the looming, black church. It appeared larger on the outside than it was.

Purposefully.

Vaslav stood on the bottom step, not quite warm enough for his liking as a light snowfall sprinkled from the sky, but this wasn't a day to complain, and he still had to greet the remaining guests.

Well, almost *all* of the guests.

Mira had already stepped beyond the front doors of the church to say hello to the three-person staff that kept the place running and maintained throughout the year. He didn't bother to check if she had already handed over the envelope he'd filled that morning meant to be a second payment; she would do her job, and quietly find a seat.

The extra money was a thank you, of sorts. One he

was sure the establishment would appreciate. Not once had they ever refused a donation from him despite being aware of the road that led Vaslav here. And all the blood he paved with it.

Despite being able to see straight through the walls, all made of glass except for the black wooden beam bones of the building and the doors, into the lobby, Vaslav focused on the establishment date that had been stamped into the step below his feet.

The *Krasota*, Beauty, was only two years old.

The crunch of tires on gravel and snow drew Vaslav's gaze upward as the first black SUV pulled beyond the gates, open for the day and wedding, at the entrance drive. Once parked, the driver exited and rounded the vehicle to open the door and extend a hand to help out his passenger.

It was only once Demyan Avdonin was satisfied his wife wasn't going to slip in the snow in her cream-colored suede boots that the two people headed Vaslav's way. Bundled in jackets with light scarves and mittens, they murmured between themselves while Claire pointed at something high on Beauty's Chapel.

The cross that stood another twenty feet higher than the sixty-foot peak.

"Wow," was the first thing Claire said.

Vaslav chuckled, glancing up at the sight himself. "Yes, she would have liked that touch, I think."

He didn't offer the two a chance to ask who the *she* in question was as they came up to the steps. Instead, he smiled and said, "I heard the architect who designed and built the place used the Thorncrown Chapel in Eureka Springs, Arkansas as inspiration for the *Krasota*."

"It almost makes you think we're going to freeze in there," the green-eyed woman said. "You know I looked this up before we came, right? Vera had the nerve to act like it wasn't a big thing."

"She's ... respectfully discreet about a lot of things."

"Too many, maybe?" Demyan asked.

Vaslav didn't think so.

"I like it that way. Anyway, the town certainly wasn't willing to refuse such a ... valuable donation," Vaslav said, choosing his words carefully in regard to the church and land that had come with it.

Vaslav figured out where Vera got her hair preening habit from when her stepmother tucked the brunette waves of her hair behind the shell of her ear, and smiled wide. Their first meeting had happened over supper the day after the couple arrived mid-week before the wedding. As sweet and kind as she was on the phone, Claire Avdonin didn't change in the presence of a man she barely knew from Adam.

She even hugged him.

Vaslav had been too shocked to hug her back.

Today would not be the same.

Coming off the remaining step, Vaslav pulled Claire in for a quick hug and a kiss on the apple of her grinning cheek. She took the greeting as gracefully as she had the one he botched on the first go-round.

"You look like you're feeling better today," she whispered as he began to pull away.

If Demyan heard the exchange, the man pretended not to notice where he stood only a foot away. His gaze fixed on the looming face of the church and how it looked surrounded by a forest of trees and an endless white sky of falling snowflakes.

"I'm hoping to get through the day," he told Claire quietly. "Plan for the worst—"

Claire smiled. "Yeah, and hope for the best, I know."

Vaslav shrugged.

That first supper at the Pashkov home had not gone as well as he meant for it to, either. But when did a night that ended with him bent over a toilet ever go as he wanted?

Claire had been kind about that, too.

"It only looks like an open-air structure," he explained. "It's heated, and thankfully, air-conditioned in the summer. Don't ask me how they clean all the windows, no?"

Demyan barked out a laugh. "A full-time job in itself, hmm?"

Vaslav nodded. "Exactly, comrade."

He extended his hand then.

Waiting for a shake.

Demyan quickly took it in his own, glancing down to see the fresh ink that was hard to miss on the back of Vaslav's hand. His old, faded spider had been turned around.

"I see you've made the choice about retirement," Demyan noted.

Vaslav dropped Demyan's hand and gestured wide. "I hear you're willing to help Igor make a … transition, no?"

The other man shrugged.

Some things didn't need to be said in the presence of a woman, and that was certainly one of them. "I think Vera will like having us here for a bit," Claire put in with a wink.

"Me, too."

Demyan pointed at his wife, asking, "I'm helping her find a seat, and then taking your spot here, yes?"

Vaslav nodded at the arriving SUV slowing for the turn at the gates. "Right, I just have to greet the other two. There's a place for your coats and things in the lobby, Claire. I'll be in shortly."

His soon-to-be in-laws, a funny concept to Vaslav considering his only other in-law had been murdered by his hand, headed up the few stone steps to the front door as the SUV came to a rolling stop directly in front of the church.

Hannah popped out of the passenger side of the vehicle, barely paying the slushy snow under her pale-yellow leather pumps any attention while Demyan and Claire stepped inside the church.

He heard Claire read out loud the plaque, written in both English and Russian, embedded under each brass door knocker before the door swung shut.

"The Beauty's Chapel - Any and All Welcome."

Even the devil needed a place to pray.

"The extra she paid for the matching cloak was *not* worth it," Hannah muttered to Vaslav and passed him by on the steps, shivering as she raced to catch up with Vera's parents. The billowing, fur-trimmed silk cloak, yellow like the floor-length soft yellow gown she held high from the wet ground, fluttered behind her, and did little to protect against the chill.

Vaslav laughed under his breath as Hannah quickly slipped beyond the doors. Turning around, he came face to face, so to speak, with the man sitting behind the driver's wheel of the SUV. Igor had rolled down the passenger side window so the two could see one another, and apparently speak.

Which would be the first time the man had talked

to Vaslav in *days*. Well, not minding business, of course. Anything else, though, Igor shut down.

His oldest friend, even if he wouldn't be able to say that forever, nodded upward at the church, leaning over the steering wheel a bit in his fitted, three-piece tux. "You know, I've never actually been inside it."

Vaslav, either.

"It's a good spot for today."

Because if Irina was in heaven, and Vaslav had to get through God to talk to her, then so be it. Had funding the cost of building the church that was practically a World Wonder in itself and donating the land and deed not been a good enough price for whatever, or whoever, *God* was?

For love, there wasn't a price Vaslav wouldn't pay.

The quiet murmur from inside the back of the SUV drew Igor's gaze over his shoulder. He rolled his eyes back to Vaslav, saying, "Someone just reminded me we have a wedding to get to."

He smirked at Vera's polite prodding.

Frankly, he'd been trying to keep his mind off the fact that she was so close, and yet, he couldn't see her. Let alone *touch* her. From the very second Igor pulled up, Vaslav was supposed to help Hannah inside, but his old friend distracted him.

"She could roll down the window."

"*Nope.*"

That time, Vera spoke loud enough for Vaslav to hear.

He chuckled darkly, shaking his head.

"You good?" Igor asked. "It's freezing."

"Are *you*?" he asked back.

That was the important question.

Because Vaslav's stance on many things, including

Kiril and his recent legal issues that had not yet been resolved, hadn't changed. The thing about people? Everybody had a line.

Igor shrugged, but his agreement came off weak all the same. "Yeah, I guess, Vas."

For today, it was his wedding day, after all, Vaslav let Igor have a pass.

"Time to get married," Demyan said as he exited the church behind Vaslav.

Right.

The only reason they were all gathered here today. Wasn't that what mattered?

*

Demyan pulled the fur-trimmed cloak from Vera's shoulders with a quick sweep of silk along her back and shoulders. Fast enough to keep any stray snowflakes from passing from the silk to her. The usher, one of three people employed by the non-profit church, stepped forward to take the item from Vera's father but other than a shift of the skirt of her dress or a peek at her hand running under her veil, the doors leading from the parish to the lobby hid her from view.

"I still think those center doors should be glass, too, no?" the minister asked behind Vaslav at the altar.

Damn near everything else was glass, side to side, back, front, and above. Spotless glass between wooden beams that crisscrossed overhead and fit together like walls that looked out into a snow-covered forest and the white canvas of the sky. Standing in the middle and staring up, it was like breathing in and then out to the world.

If God wasn't here, peace sure was.

"I didn't build the damn thing, David," Vaslav said.

Just paid for it.

"Of course, you're right."

Thankfully, the man quieted when the latches on the door handles at the far end of the black-stained hardwood aisle rattled. Only thirty feet in length, with double rows of bench pews cushioned with crushed black velvet every three feet on either side, Vera didn't have far to walk to him once she was beyond the doors.

In his mind, it took ages.

He hoped that meant he wouldn't soon forget the sight of Vera when she did finally step through the doors with her father at her side. The knee-length lace veil kept even her face from his view, except for the swath of red that painted her lips a bright hue behind the haze of white. Far longer in the back, the veil fell like a train down to the floor.

She kept both hands tucked together at her father's elbow and leaned her head Demyan's way when he smiled. His lips moved with words Vaslav and the handful of people at the front of the church couldn't hear.

Everything about the day had been easy because Vera made it that way. She didn't fuss, barely asked for anything to be happy to smile, and hadn't even bothered with a bouquet of flowers. What she wanted, she had told Vaslav in bed late the night before after days of snide silence and stubborn hearts between them, was him.

Just him.

Waiting at the end.

So, he was.

For love, it seemed like an easy trade.

*

Dearest readers,

It's been a trip—a whole journey, really—to get Vas and Vera to this point. I hope you're ready for the final book in their saga …

The Breath Before Forever, coming very, *very* soon.

Xo,
BK

ABOUT THE AUTHOR

The author of too many novels to count, Bethany-Kris is a Canadian, lover of much, and mother to four sons, a glaring of cats, and a pack of dogs. A small town in Eastern Canada where she was born and raised is where she has always called home. With her boys under her feet, a snuggling cat, barking dogs, and a spouse calling over his shoulder, she is nearly always writing something ... when she can find the time.

Find where to follow BK and keep up to date with all her book news at www.bethanykris.com.

OTHER BOOKS

The Beast of Moscow Saga

The Beast of Moscow
The Lies Between Lovers
The Beauty Who Loved Him
The Breath Before Forever

The Darkest Lies Trilogy

The Agreement
The Promise
The Marriage

After Another Trilogy

One Step After Another
One Breath After Another
One Second After Another

Boykov Bratva

Fractured Ties
Essence of Fear

The Guzzi Legacy

Corrado
Alessio
Chris
Beni
Bene
Marcus
The Firsts: A Guzzi Legacy Companion Novel
The Guzzi Legacy: Vol 1
The Guzzi Legacy: Vol 2

Renzo + Lucia

Privilege
Harbor
Contempt
Forever
Cusp
Renzo + Lucia: The Complete Trilogy

Andino + Haven

Duty
Vow
One Last Time
Andino + Haven: The Complete Duet

John + Siena

Loyalty
Disgrace
John + Siena: The Complete Duet
John + Siena: Extended

Cross + Catherine

Always
Revere
Unruly
The Companion
Naz & Roz

Guzzi Duet

Unraveled, Book One
Entangled, Book Two
Cara & Gian: The Complete Duet

DeLuca Duet

Waste of Worth: Part One
Worth of Waste: Part Two

Standalone Titles

Pink
Pretty Lies
Dirty Pool
Effortless
Inflict
Cozen
Captivated
Dishonored

Donati Bloodlines

Thin Lies
Thin Lines
Thin Lives
Behind the Bloodlines
The Complete Trilogy

Filthy Marcellos

Antony
Lucian
Giovanni
Dante
Legacy
A Very Marcello Christmas
The Complete Collection

Seasons of Betrayal

Where the Sun Hides
Where the Snow Falls
Where the Wind Whispers
Seasons: The Complete Seasons of Betrayal Series

Gun Moll Trilogy

Gun Moll
Gangster Moll
Madame Moll

The Chicago War

Deathless & Divided
Reckless & Ruined
Scarless & Sacred
Breathless & Bloodstained
The Complete Series
Maldives & Mistletoe

The Russian Guns

The Arrangement
The Life
The Score
Demyan & Ana
Shattered
The Jersey Vignettes

FANTASY ROMANCE

The Hunted: A 9INE REALMS Novel

Find more on Bethany-Kris's website at
www.bethanykris.com.